**Lori sti...**
**dreamy ...**
**waiting f...**

Her body was taut, aching for his touch, and she didn't want the feeling to slip away. What she wanted was to feel him all over her, inside her, tasting and teasing and probing places that were in desperate need of attention.

*What the hell? How far can things go inside my garage?* she rationalized, arching forward and flattening her breasts against his chest while stifling the moan of joy that crept into her throat. She let him push her back against the car, inviting Ramon to press closer and devour her mouth in a deep, probing kiss. As their tongues explored and flicked over each other's in their search for satisfaction, Ramon's fingers worked on the knot in the straps that held Lori's halter top in place. When the soft white fabric fell to her waist, Lori gulped back her need, parted her legs and guided Ramon to stand between them.

She welcomed the feel of his tongue and the scorch of his fingers, loving the blistering press of his ample size as it grew hard against the flat of her stomach.

"Hey, Lori!" Brittany's voice bounced against the closed garage door and jolted Lori out of her self-indulgent trance. "Oh, my God! It's my neighbor," Lori hissed, forcing Ramon to back away so she could pull up her halter top and retie the straps.

"Not a word," she whispered to Ramon as she pressed the button to raise the garage door, pushing an explosion of black curls out of her eyes.

**Books by Anita Bunkley**

Kimani Romance

*Suite Embrace*
*Suite Temptation*
*Spotlight on Desire*
*Vote for Love*
*First Class Seduction*

---

## ANITA BUNKLEY

is the author of many successful mainstream novels and novellas and enjoys writing romance for her many fans. A member of the Texas Institute of Letters and an NAACP Image Award nominee, she is a recipient of a 2007 Career Achievement Award from *RT Book Reviews*. Anita lives in Houston, Texas, with her husband, Crawford.

# *First Class* SEDUCTION

## ANITA BUNKLEY

KIMANI
ROMANCE

To my husband, Crawford, with love.

 KIMANI PRESS™

Recycling programs
for this product may
not exist in your area.

ISBN-13: 978-0-373-86165-1

FIRST CLASS SEDUCTION

Dear Reader,

As an avid traveler, I often wondered just how exciting the life of an airline flight attendant could be. While preparing for this story, I spent some time chatting with a friend of mine who works for a major airline as an attendant. She agreed that her job can be very stressful at times, but meeting so many people from different cultures and nations is indeed a wonderful adventure.

While traveling, I love to observe fellow passengers, trying to guess where people are going, who their companions are and why they are taking a particular flight. My idea for *First Class Seduction* came to me during a recent flight to Italy as I watched a handsome man flirt openly with our very attractive flight attendant. When we arrived in Rome and departed the airport, I wondered if the two managed to get together. I hope so, as they made a very strong impression on me…and several other passengers!

Drawing story lines from real-life experiences is what I love to do, and I keep my eyes and ears on alert for any spark that can inspire my next romantic story. Living on the Texas Gulf Coast with Mexico as a close neighbor also inspired me to create this intercultural love story. I hope you enjoy my romance of flight and intrigue as we cross geographical borders and see love bloom between two very special characters.

If you love to travel, crave adventure and like a bit of mystery, this is the book for you.

If you want to drop me a line, please e-mail me at arbun@sbcglobal.net.

Read with love!

Anita Bunkley

# Chapter 1

Lori Myles finished her virgin strawberry daiquiri, slipped off her barstool, tugged down the hem of her ruffled miniskirt and accepted the stranger's outstretched hand. Moving with precise steps in her black stilettos, she followed her new dance partner into the pulsing throng that was grinding and bumping to Usher's latest single on Club Azule's too-small dance floor.

The club, named for its spectacular view of Acapulco Bay, was a popular "in" spot in the resort town's throbbing nightclub scene. The exclusive nightspot, tucked away on a quiet curve of the bay, dished out music that drew locals as well as tourists who wanted to socialize, enjoy the music and dance the night away.

Whirling strobe lights flashed overhead and cool neon color beams glowed in the semidark, providing Lori with a fractured glimpse of the man who was guiding her into the gyrating mob. He was slim, but his tight booty was high, round and encased in fitted jeans. His V-shaped torso, flanked by muscular arms that bulged impressively under a short-sleeved polo shirt, tapered into a wide leather belt studded with silver nails. His wavy black hair swept the ridge of solid shoulders as his slight jerk of a swagger sent the teardrop earring in his right earlobe into a dance of its own. As each burst from the strobe lights hit his golden brown skin, he glowed like copper money.

As soon as her partner elbowed space for them in the frenzied crowd, the music suddenly shifted from Usher's fast-paced beat to a sensuous number by Mary J. Blige, changing the mood entirely. Some couples left the dance floor. Others slid into place, arms wrapped around each other to execute slow, sexy moves.

Lori gave her partner a quizzical look, wondering if he still wanted to dance. He responded by taking her hand and easing her into position, his arm circling her waist. She dropped her shoulders, sucked in a silent breath and tightened her grip on him, surprisingly shaken by the way his probing dark eyes were boring into her. Something told her that this man wanted to show off his stuff, and she planned to match him step for step.

Biting back a satisfied smile, Lori followed his lead, impressed by the near-perfect moves he was throwing down. In her opinion, this was the best way to spend a free evening—in the arms of a handsome stranger who was all about the music and the moves, and not into a lot of disjointed, phony conversation that served no purpose and went nowhere. She did not go to clubs to meet men, but to dance, and this guy was one smooth operator. He had not uttered a single word.

*Fine with me,* Lori thought, appreciating his lack of conversation. She spoke Spanish well enough, but rarely spoke to the men she danced with. No English was the best route to take. That way there were no complications, no false promises or drama, only a good time and a fast exit when it was time to leave.

At twenty-nine, Lori had worked for Globus-Americas Airlines (GAA) for six years, with a flying schedule that took her from Houston to Mexico City, and then on to Acapulco—a dream of a schedule that fit her carefree lifestyle as well as her love of travel and adventure. An avid dancer, Lori had come to Club Azule to escape her hotel and spend a few hours of her overnight layover having fun in Acapulco. Working as a flight attendant for GAA was exciting, but stressful work, and dancing was a good way to wind down after her long flight. Keeping things impersonal, uncomplicated, and stress-free was the only way to go. For her, a perfect night out meant bumping and grinding to music with someone who had no interest in anything other than a good time. Someone who shunned name-giving, requests for cell phone numbers, and questions about her plans for tomorrow. Why bother with all that nonproductive talk? By tomorrow morning, she'd be high in the sky, flying away from Acapulco, and on her way back to Houston.

When Mary J hit a high, soulful note and ended the set, Lori stepped out of her partner's arms, nodded her thanks and turned to walk away. However, she was jolted to a halt when he tightened his hold on her hand and forced her to look at him.

"Thank you for the dance. It was beautiful," he said in flawless English that had no trace of a Spanish accent. "You're the most beautiful woman here tonight. And a hell of a dancer, too."

His melodious voice, his gentlemanly manner and his striking good looks made Lori's heart turn over. He sounded sincere, as if he actually expected her to be impressed by his words of praise. She tried to suppress a smile, but failed. Grinning at him, she lifted her chin, blinked her acknowledgment and started to pivot away, but he pulled her forward, placed two fingers beneath her chin and raised her mouth to his. Instinctively, Lori backed away, but when he leaned in and pressed a firm kiss on her lips, she froze. A buzz of heat flashed through Lori, carrying a warning signal to the rational part of her brain, which her lips obviously ignored. When her tongue touched his, the kiss intensified, and Lori sank into it with little hesitation, as if accepting a souvenir of her evening at Club Azule.

Standing on a dance floor in Acapulco and kissing a stranger—that was the craziest thing she'd ever done. But it seemed so natural. Why? She worried as the kiss broke off almost as quickly as it started.

Without a word, her handsome dance partner slipped into the crowd, leaving Lori to watch him go. He walked with his head tilted back, his shoulders high, as if he owned the world. As if he did as he pleased and got whatever he wanted, she thought. Hadn't he just proven that by the moves he'd made on her? Lori could still feel his black eyes caressing her face and his muscular brown arms holding her close, and was oh-so-tempted to go after him. Just to talk to him. To find out who he was, and when he'd be at the club again.

*But why bother?* she decided. *This has been fun, but it's time to go back to the hotel and forget this ever happened. He's long gone, anyway.*

Shaking off crazy thoughts of seeking out her mystery man, Lori went back to her seat at the bar to settle her bill, but before she could ask for it, a mature man wearing a white suit and a charming smile offered her his hand. Lori checked her watch.

*One last dance before shutting down for the night,* she told herself. *Exactly what I need to shake off that last go-round.*

With a flip of her hair and a wide smile of greeting, Lori stepped into a hot salsa number with her new partner, wrapping her mind around her early call tomorrow morning instead of the kissing stranger she would never see again.

From the opposite side of the dance floor, Ramón Vidal watched Lori execute a sensuous salsa routine with her new partner. A shimmer of interest slid through him, making it impossible for him to tear his eyes off the woman who was not like any he'd ever met at the club before. Her silky tan skin reminded him of sweet almonds. Her dark hair, flying free as she swung from side to side, created a sensuous frame around her heart-stopping face. Luscious full lips called to him from across the room, begging for another kiss, and her sexy round hips, swinging with the beat of the music, initiated surges of desire—and even jealousy.

*Why do I feel like I want to get close to her?* he wondered. He didn't even know the woman's name, let alone have any claim to her. He never picked up girls in clubs, and tonight would be no exception. With a flip of his wrist, Ramón slapped a $20 bill down on the bar and squeezed his way through the crowded club to the front door. Once outside, he took a long breath to clear his head. Staring across the dark waters of Acapulco Bay, he swept two fingers across lips that still burned from the luscious hot kiss he'd just shared with a stranger. A beautiful stranger whose touch had sparked jolts of desire that both disturbed and excited Ramón.

## Chapter 2

Though it was six o'clock in the morning, Lori awoke alert and energized despite her late night out. Since she never drank alcohol while on the job, tired feet were usually the only reminders of the fun she'd had the night before. Eager to get on with her day, Lori took a hot shower, applied the minimal makeup that kept her morning routine easy—mascara, blush and a little lip gloss—secured her long black hair into a fancy twist to keep it off her face and then snapped her suitcase closed.

Wearing her navy blue and red GAA uniform, she rolled her flight bag into the elevator and across the hotel lobby, where she dropped her room key into the fast checkout and exited through the sliding-glass doors.

Outside the hotel, a white van was waiting to take the flight crew to the airport. Since Lori was the first to arrive, she settled into a seat in the middle row and stared out the window, fingertips at her lips, her mind returning to the gorgeous guy whose mini-seduction had left her wanting more. After her final turn on the dance floor, she'd looked around the club on her way out, hoping to see him one more time. However, he had vanished as quickly as he'd appeared, like the seagulls that swooped out over the bay and slipped into the swirling clouds.

Tilting her head back against the seat, Lori closed her eyes, slightly uneasy with the thought that she actually hoped to run into her mystery kisser when she returned to Acapulco. Why was her mind so crowded with thoughts of that guy? All he had done was kiss her. Besides, bringing a new man into her life was not on her social agenda. As far as Lori was concerned, a committed relationship would compromise her independence and complicate her fast-paced schedule.

The alarming experience she'd had with her last boyfriend had cured Lori of making impulsive, emotional moves. Devan Parker's face flashed into Lori's mind. He was the man who'd cemented her vow never to get tangled up in a serious relationship with someone she barely knew.

Last year, when Lori met Devan in the elevator at the airport parking garage in Houston, she'd smiled at the handsome brother wearing a sharp pinstriped suit when he pushed the Down button for her. At five in the morning, she'd been rushing to check in for work, with a cup of coffee in one hand and her rolling bag handle in the other. He'd been hurrying to catch a flight to Los Angeles.

Devan's earthy cologne had filled the elevator with an intoxicating scent that pushed Lori's interest into overdrive. He was the most attractive, polite and sexy-looking man she had met in quite a while, and by the time the elevator reached the terminal, she'd handed him her business card and had taken his.

Three days later, Devan sent her a text message, asking Lori to meet him for lunch at the Italian restaurant inside the Marriott Hotel near the airport. She agreed, and at warp speed, they tumbled headfirst into a relationship that exploded with adventuresome sex, fancy dates at trendy clubs and silly fun days just hanging out in the city. Devan infused Lori's tightly scheduled life with excitement, and she willingly allowed him to consume every minute of her free time. Falling for Devan had happened so quickly and so easily, she should have known the affair wouldn't last…or end as smoothly as she'd hoped.

"Hey, early bird," Phyllis Marshall called out, climbing into the van, followed by Sam and Allen, fellow crew members who were also juggling cups and navy blue flight bags.

"Up and out, that's me," Lori joked, mentally closing the door on the past to zero in on the long workday that lay ahead.

"What time did you get back last night?" Phyllis inquired, stowing her bag in the luggage rack at the front of the vehicle before focusing on Lori.

"A little after twelve," Lori replied, scooting over to make room for Phyllis to sit beside her, while the two male flight attendants settled into seats in the rear.

"I don't see how you do it," Phyllis remarked, stifling a yawn. "I went to bed at nine and still, could have used a few more hours in the sack."

Lori shrugged and raised a brow at Phyllis, who at fifty-one, was the senior flight attendant and self-proclaimed mother hen of the crew. Her salt-and-pepper hair, wise blue eyes and authoritative voice inspired respect and trust. When Phyllis doled out her motherly advice, her much younger crew members usually listened, convinced that she cared about them and would have their backs if things got rough. At her age, and after a long career with GAA, Phyllis knew the business well and was generous in her support.

"Hotel rooms bore me," Lori responded in her defense. "I can only take them for so long and then I have to get out and check out the local scene. Watching TV and eating room service meals drive me nuts. Dancing relaxes me. It's like a good workout, only much more fun."

A flicker of her bright blue eyes was all that Phyllis offered.

"You could have come to the soccer game with me and Sam," Allen called up from the back of the van. "The fans in this town are absolutely wild. I was beginning to think we might not make it out of the stadium alive when the home team lost. Hell, it was a mob scene in there!"

While the two guys discussed the soccer game they'd attended the night before, Lori turned back to Phyllis. "You should have come. I found a great club on the beach. It had walls of glass and a fabulous view of the ocean. Really a spectacular place. The men here really know how to dance," Lori said, giving Phyllis a brief overview of her night out on the town, but omitting the fact that her Latin dance partner had kissed her and then disappeared.

Phyllis, who rarely ventured out of her hotel during layovers, made a sound in her throat that told Lori she was not particularly impressed by her coworker's description of her latest layover adventure.

"You need to be more careful," Phyllis warned. "American women out alone are targets for all kinds of scams and dangerous schemes. What do you get out of going to those clubs, anyway?"

"A good time," Lori answered, not particularly worried about Phyllis's concerns. Lori had chosen a career as a flight attendant so she could travel, meet new people, experience different cultures. Hiding out in fear in a hotel room when she could enjoy one of the most beautiful cities in the world was not her idea of fun. "Besides, I can protect myself," Lori went on, turning from Phyllis to look straight ahead as the van pulled onto the highway leading to the airport. "I have a black belt in karate, remember?"

"What good is that if some man puts a drug in your drink? Takes you away in his car and you wind up getting raped, beaten or left alone in some strange place?"

Lori's head whipped around, jaw raised as she shook her head in disbelief. "Really, Phyllis! You need to stop. Nothing like that will ever happen to me."

"How do you know? It could. Happens all the time. There was a story on Worldwide News last night about a woman in Brazil who…" Phyllis persisted, rattling on about a bizarre tale of drugs, international kidnapping and identity theft that she had seen on TV the night before.

"You've been watching too many true-crime programs," Lori commented with a flip of her hand.

Phyllis made a grunt in response and went on. "Criminals make a lot of money off naive people who don't pay attention to what's going on around them. Million-dollar ransoms are common," she finished, pressing her lips into a hard line to emphasize her point.

"Maybe," Lori hedged, not wanting to get into a back-and-forth with her coworker over a hypothetical situation. "But I don't make enough money to be a target for anything other than a spin on the dance floor," she admitted to Phyllis.

*But I sure would love to feel my mystery kisser's arms around me again,* Lori thought, wishing she'd bent her rules at Club Azule and gotten personal with her Latin hunk.

# Chapter 3

When the sleek black Mercedes pulled up to the Passenger Drop-off area at Mexico National Airport, Ramón turned in his seat and faced his brother, Xavier, who put the car in Park.

"Congratulations again, bro," Ramón said to Xavier, flashing a proud smile at his elder, and only, sibling. "You're gonna be the best judge in the state of Guerrero," Ramón predicted. "Probably make it to the Mexican Supreme Court one day."

Xavier Vidal assessed his brother's face with a steady, solemn gaze. "That is definitely part of my plan," he stated with the kind of confidence that validated Ramón's prediction.

At forty-two, Xavier was ten years older than Ramón, but the two brothers were very close. Their parents had emigrated from rural Mexico to the United States when Xavier was five years old, becoming U.S. citizens by the time Ramón was born in Houston five years later. After graduating from law school at the University of Texas, Xavier returned to Mexico to open a law practice in Acapulco, leaving his baby brother behind.

"Thanks for coming down for my swearing-in ceremony," Xavier said, placing a hand on Ramón's shoulder.

"Wouldn't have missed it for the world. Only wish Dad could've come with me," Ramón replied, swallowing the emotional lump that rose in this throat as he recalled his father's disappointment when Ramón insisted that he stay home.

At sixty-one, Tomás Vidal, who had suffered two heart attacks in the past four years, resided in an assisted living center near Ramón's condo in Houston. Ramón visited his dad every day, made sure he had everything he needed and kept him up-to-date on family news. Since Ramón and Xavier were all the immediate family that Tomás now had, the three Vidal men were very close.

"I know Pop was upset, but his heart was so weak that any travel is too risky," Xavier agreed.

"Yeah, but it's so hard for him to accept."

"I know… I'm glad you live close enough to keep an eye on him."

"Dinner once a week at Hugo's. No exceptions or excuses allowed." Ramón laughed.

"I know he loves that," Xavier replied.

"He does. And as soon as we sit down at his favorite table, his face lights up. He even flirts with the waitresses."

Xavier grinned, slapped Ramón on the arm, and said, "Well, give him my love. I'll call next week, after things settle down."

"Will do." Ramón reached around, grabbed his carry-on bag off the back seat, and patted the outside pocket. "I got your swearing-in ceremony right here on DVD, so Pop can see you taking your oath of office." Ramón shook his head and chuckled under his breath. "He'll probably invite everyone in the center over to his room to watch this with him. He's very proud of you… and so am I."

Xavier nodded, lips compressed in understanding. "Well, next time you come to Acapulco, you've gotta stay at the house."

"I will. I promise."

"And we'll spend some time just hanging out," Xavier added. "Sorry I couldn't hit the club with you last night, but with all the people in town, and the crowd at the house…"

"No problem," Ramón interrupted, knowing that Xavier had been swept up in a whirlwind of congratulatory lunches, dinners and parties all weekend. "I understand, bro. Not much was happening at Azule anyway."

The blast of a taxi driver's horn alerted Xavier that he had been at the Drop-off stand longer than allowed. "Hey. Gotta go," he said to Ramón, who quickly opened the passenger-side door. "I'm blocking traffic and you're gonna miss your flight. Later!"

"Yeah, later!" Ramón echoed. He shook his brother's hand, got out and slammed the car door shut, but remained at the curb as Xavier nudged his luxury car into the long line of vehicles clogging the exit from Mexico National Airport.

Ramón adjusted his sunglasses and thought about his comment on the club scene last night. *Not much was happening at Club Azule.* Really? If that was the case, why did his encounter with the most attractive and intriguing woman he had ever danced with keep flashing like a Technicolor video in his brain?

Ramón turned and headed into the terminal, thinking about the weekend, glad he'd made the trip to see Xavier take an honored place in Mexico's judicial system.

"Good for him," Ramón murmured to himself, a deep sense of satisfaction coming over him. He admired his older brother very much, and the age gap between the two had seemed to narrow over the years. It was as if the older they got, the closer they became, and now, even though they lived more than a thousand miles apart, they talked, texted or e-mailed each other almost every day.

Just as he entered the terminal, Ramón's cell phone rang, breaking into his mental musing. Checking the phone's screen, he saw that Keith Harris, his business partner in Houston, was calling. Punching the trackball, he greeted Keith, and was upset to hear that the installation of a security system for a major furniture retailer in Dallas was a week behind schedule. As the co-owner of the high-tech security company, Vida-Shield, Ramón was constantly putting out fires.

"Who's at fault—the site foreman or the supplier?" Ramón asked Keith, pissed off that one of his most complicated jobs was only half finished and already over budget.

"Both," Keith replied.

"Need me to fly straight into Dallas, instead of coming home?" Ramón asked, knowing he could not let this situation deteriorate any further.

"No," Keith said. "I'm on my way up there now. I'll check in after I get a handle on what's happening."

"Good. I'm about to board my plane. I'll call as soon as I land," Ramón replied, thankful that he had such a competent and trustworthy business partner.

Inside the terminal building, Ramón scanned the flight board for the gate number for Globus-Americas Airlines flight 565, eager to get home to Houston and back to work. Maybe then, he'd be able to get last night's dance-floor kiss out of his mind.

# *Chapter 4*

Moving up from the rear of the plane with an armload of pillows, Lori left her fellow crewmembers, Sam and Allen, hanging out in the back to monitor the dwindling space in the overhead bins. She squeezed past passengers stuffing bags of all shapes and sizes into the narrow bins, knowing that space was going quickly. Soon, leftover bags would need to be checked back at the plane's main cabin door, tensions would begin to mount and wrestling oversized duffel bags from surly passengers would begin. However, the one-hour, fifty-five minute flight from Acapulco to Houston, with a short stop in Mexico City, would give everyone plenty of time to calm down.

Boarding always produced the most problems, snafus and complaints during a flight, stressing out the flight attendants, whose main goal was to get carry-ons stowed and everyone seated as quickly as possible so the captain could depart on time.

As soon as Lori reached the first-class cabin, she handed the pillows to a family of four seated in the last two rows and then took their drink requests. Two sodas for the kids and two champagne mimosas for the parents. Lori nodded her understanding at the harried-looking mother who seemed to have struggled to get her sullen preteens settled into their seats.

While Phyllis prepared the drinks, Lori approached passengers seated in the emergency exit rows to determine if they were willing and able to assist in case of an emergency. Even though one of the passengers was quite elderly, the wiry little man assured Lori that he was up to the task.

When Lori returned to the first-class cabin, she met the agent working the flight. The agent handed her a copy of the manifest, which listed first-class passengers, passengers with special needs or meals, and any gate connections. She glanced at it, turned to face the passengers seated in the forward cabin and started her walk-through to get a head count.

However, she had not taken two full steps when she froze in the center aisle, her eyes riveted on the man sitting by the window in row 2, seat A. Was it possible? Was that her mysterious dance partner from the night before, calmly leafing through a magazine? Quickly, she checked the passenger list. Ramón Vidal—destination: Houston, Texas. Squinting at him, she did a double take. Yes, he was the man who'd burned her lips with his fiery kiss and branded her heart with an ache that wouldn't go away.

Drawing in a calming breath, she moved right up to the edge of his seat to make sure he saw her. "Well, hello," Lori said, trying to sound as casual as if she'd just run into a classmate from her college days, aware that everyone in first class would hear every word she said.

Ramón lifted his head, slid his sexy brown eyes up to hers and then hit her with the most adorable half smile Lori had ever seen, making her body tense and her nerve endings flare.

"Well…hi. You work here?" Ramón asked, looking bewildered as he glanced around, half turning in his seat.

"That's right. I'm Lori, your flight attendant and I'll be taking care of you during our flight to Houston." Even though the plane hadn't left the tarmac yet, her insides were tumbling around as if they'd entered a rough patch of turbulence. She held on to the nearest seat back to maintain her balance and looked down at the manifest again, determined to hold her emotions together. "Uh, so, you're Mr. Vidal, right?" she inquired, shifting her attention back to Ramón, thankful that no one was sitting beside him.

"Yes, that's me…but you can call me Ramón," he offered, giving Lori a wink that revved her pulse like a jet engine preparing to take off.

"Would you like something to drink?" she asked, slipping into her perkiest passenger-request mode, knowing she couldn't ask him what was really zipping through her brain: *Why did you kiss me and disappear? Why did you have to wind up on my flight? Why are you making me so damn nervous? Would you like to go dancing again?*

"Oh…sure. Coffee. Black." Ramón paused, reconsidered and then added, "And a Bloody Mary, too. Extra spicy." He lifted his index finger, as if to stop her from moving on, his half grin exploding into a full-blown smile. "I hope you enjoyed yourself at the club last night. I sure did." He rested his head against the back of his seat. A glittering ray of sunlight streamed through the cabin window and lit the teardrop earring in his left ear.

"Yes, I did have a good time," Lori murmured, not about to expand on the topic as she pivoted away from Ramón and turned to the passengers across the aisle.

"Would you like something to drink?" she asked the Middle Eastern couple sitting across from Ramón. As soon as they'd given Lori their order, Ramón leaned across the empty seat next to him and forced Lori to glance back.

"So, you're gonna give me first-class service all the way, right?" he teasingly called over to her.

Lori sent a scowl of warning at Ramón, whose sensuous expression was begging her to forget about helping the other passengers and sit down beside him so they could chat. But that would never happen. She had too much to do to let him become a distraction.

"Yes, sir, first-class service all the way," Lori replied with a mental jerk, her words clipped and tight. "If you need anything at all during the flight, Mr. Vidal, don't hesitate to ask," she finished, ignoring his request for her to call him by his first name. "Globus-Americas wants you to be as comfortable as possible."

"Thanks, I'm sure you'll do everything to my satisfaction," he assured her, pinning Lori with that same dark look he'd zapped her with in Club Azule.

Once they were airborne, Lori got busy serving passengers, but couldn't escape Ramón's insistent attempts to monopolize her attention. If she paused by his seat, he made some remark about his love of Acapulco and how much he looked forward to visiting the city again. When she bent down to hand him a drink, he would add a tidbit about some place she should try to see the next time she was there. As she walked up and down the aisle during meal service, he had no problem stopping to make some new request. Another Bloody Mary. A more interesting magazine. A pillow, please? More coffee. Help with the earpiece before the movie came on.

As the miles slipped by and the plane zoomed toward Houston, Lori grew more and more irritated, yet intrigued, by the man who seemed to want to become her new best friend. *Or more than that,* she decided, amused with his determination to attract her attention and occupy her time.

Deep into the flight, Phyllis squeezed past Lori with a food tray and threw her a What-in-the-world-is-going-on? kind of look. Lori cut her eyes and jerked her head toward the galley, where she cornered Phyllis and confessed everything. "That's one of the guys I danced with at the club last night. We danced and then…well, he kissed me and walked away."

"Kissed you and disappeared?" Phyllis probed, touching her tongue to her upper lip as she refilled a coffee cup for the father of the still-sulking preteens. "Come on, Lori. More than a dance and a kiss must have happened," Phyllis said. "Mr. Vidal is practically undressing you with those gorgeous brown eyes, and anyone looking at him can tell the guy is totally smitten with you. What went on that you aren't telling me?"

"Nothing else, I promise," Lori groaned, placing china and

glassware on a tray. "And the kiss was not that much of a deal, really. Anyway, I never thought I'd see him again."

"But there he is, chatting you up and feeling you up with his eyes."

"Kinda looks that way, huh?" Lori admitted, feeling as if Ramón Vidal were still staring at her.

"Damn straight. So what are you going to do?"

"About what?" Lori tossed back.

"About him! I have to admit he is kinda sexy. Why don't you find out what you can about him while you have him captive?"

"Absolutely not. I'm not going to go out there and grill him for information."

"Oh, go on. Just talk to him. He might be a keeper."

Lori snapped a white linen napkin at Phyllis, like a punctuation mark to end their conversation. "Please. I am not looking for a keeper and you know it."

"Hey, don't be so sure. Everybody needs somebody, sometime, Miss Play-the-Field. I've been widowed for ten years, but I knew what it was like to have a good man in my life. You deserve that, too."

"I'm not about to rush things."

"I understand your concern about getting involved again after what you went through with Devan Parker, but your I-don't-want-to-be-attached attitude ought to be wearing thin by now. Go on. Your mystery man is so eager to talk… See what you can find out about him."

Muttering an unintelligible reply, Lori finished preparing her tray and then headed out to serve her passengers.

Once food service ended, the crew tidied the cabin and dimmed the lights for in-flight movie and TV-watching. Taking advantage of the break, Lori returned to the forward galley to stash supplies while Phyllis headed to the rear of the plane to see if the guys in the back needed help getting their passengers settled in for the rest of the flight.

"Mind if I stand here and stretch my legs for a minute?"

Lori's head whipped around. "Oh. No," she told Ramón, not totally surprised to see him standing in the galley entry, coffee cup in hand. "Be my guest," she added. "It's a good idea to get up and walk around."

"I don't know about walking around…all I want to do is stay right here and talk to you." His velvet-smooth voice was low and controlled.

"Yeah? About what?" Lori asked in a flirtatious manner, deciding that Phyllis might be right. Maybe it was time to put old fears behind her and stop throwing roadblocks in front of every man who threw out a pickup line.

The hum of the jet engines filled the silence as Ramón considered how to answer. He wanted Lori to talk about herself—to tell him what she liked, what she wanted, what his chances were of getting closer to her. But why would she tell all to a stranger she'd only just met in a club the night before? No, the best way to get her to open up was for him to open up first.

"Why don't I tell you a little about myself?" he started, taking the easiest route.

Lori shut the door to the microwave oven, nodded her approval and smiled. "Sure. What would you like me to know about you?"

"That I'm single, straight, and I work hard every day."

"Oh? Doing what?" Lori asked.

"Keeping people safe," Ramón replied.

"Interesting. Were you in Mexico on vacation?"

"No, visiting my brother, Xavier. He's just become a district judge in the state of Guerrero."

"Good for him. So your brother lives in Acapulco?" Lori asked.

"Right. In a spectacular house on the bay."

"Then you're…I guess…you're Mexican?"

Ramón chuckled at Lori's hesitation to probe deeper into his ethnicity. His bronze skin, dark wavy hair and lack of an accent often left people confused about where he was from. While growing up in Houston, classmates and teachers had called him everything from mixed-race black, to Italian and even Middle

Eastern, and he had learned over the years not to take offense, but to speak with pride about his Mexican-American heritage.

"Born and raised in Texas. My parents emigrated to the United States from Mexico and became naturalized citizens before I was born. My mom passed away a few years back, but my dad still lives in Houston. Only a few miles from me."

"You said something about keeping people safe. Are you a policeman?" Lori asked.

"No, I own a security company. Alarms, burglar systems, that kind of stuff. It's called Vida-Shield Security. My partner and I specialize in state-of-the-art systems for residences, businesses and government agencies."

"So...if I ever needed protection, you'd be the one to call?" Lori joked.

"Absolutely. Here's my card. As it says right there... We're experts at keeping strangers out of your home."

"That's funny," Lori tossed back, chuckling softly as she scanned his business card and read from it, "Let the experts keep strangers out of your home." Again, a low laugh escaped her throat.

Her humorous response took Ramón by surprise, and he watched her closely as he asked, "What's so funny about alarm systems, burglar bars and passcodes to stop criminals in their tracks?"

"Oh, it's not that. It's just that Globus-Americas' motto is, "'We're experts at making strangers feel at home.'"

Ramón fingered his earring, smiling. *I'd sure like to let her make me feel at home,* he thought, determined to make headway while he had the chance because once they landed, they would go their separate ways and maybe never see each other again. He had to make an impression that would last beyond the moment the plane hit the ground. "Well, I can certainly testify that you do your job well," he replied. "And I hope we won't be strangers very long."

Lori gave him a look that sent a ripple of anticipation through Ramón when she tossed her head back and tucked his card into the skirt pocket of her uniform. "Never know when I might need a safety check," she teased, breaking the sexual tension that was connecting them like an invisible length of wire.

Ramón stepped closer to Lori, filling the tiny galley with his frame and blocking her from leaving. Attracting women had never been a problem for Ramón, but he was very choosy about the ones he dated. He didn't go out a lot, but when he did, he made sure he spent time with women who intrigued, attracted and impressed him. Lori did all three, in a big way, and getting to know her was going to be a pleasure. He placed two fingers on the side of Lori's neck, bent down and brushed his lips over hers. "I can't think of anything I'd enjoy more than keeping a woman like you safe from harm."

# Chapter 5

Twin rock waterfalls on either side of the entry to Brightwood Estates welcomed Lori home. As she drove up the cedar-lined road that wound its way toward her house, she admired the meticulous landscaping of her subdivision. Passing blooming oleanders, vibrant crepe myrtles and colorful hibiscus as large as dinner plates, she congratulated herself once again on buying her house when she did, because real estate prices had soared in the past four years. Five minutes from Bush Intercontinental Airport, her neighborhood was convenient, quiet and strategically located near one of north Houston's largest shopping malls.

Lori swung into the driveway of her two-story, Tuscan-style home and beeped her horn at Brittany Adams, her next-door neighbor, who was outside clipping roses from the bright pink bushes blossoming in front of her mini-French chateau.

Brittany had become Lori's friend as soon as the two women met and discovered that they were sorority sisters. Brittany was a former teenage TV celebrity who had starred in a black family sitcom similar to the *Cosby* show. Cast as a sassy, smart, but devious teenager, she had helped push the sitcom to number one in the ratings with her crazy antics, near-potty-mouth one-liners, and troublemaking schemes. However, the show ran its course, and was canceled, throwing sixteen-year-old Brittany into a tailspin that left her confused, drug-addicted and broke. A six-month stint in rehab ended her dependence on prescription painkillers. After winning a nasty lawsuit against her stepfather/manager, she left Hollywood for Houston with a hefty bank account, determined to live a "normal" life.

Now, at thirty, Brittany was no longer the gawky teenager with braces and corkscrew curls who had exploded on the small screen with an angelic brown face and a tongue as tart as acid. Leaving Hollywood, she had gone to great lengths to transform her looks so that no one would ever recognize her as the child star gone wild, and she loved the anonymity that came with her new life. Now she was a stylishly slim, mature young woman who sported a chic short hairstyle, designer jeans and beaded T-shirts, even to do her gardening. She lived very well off her syndication royalties, shopped at high-end stores, drove a silver Jag and insisted that her California rat-race lifestyle was behind her, even though she was writing the pilot for a show about a female detective—a series in which she hoped to star.

"Hey, how's it going, Brit?" Lori called over after lowering her window. "Your roses are beautiful, as always. My mother would be so envious. Her roses aren't doing that well this year."

Brittany clipped one more bud, waved it at Lori, and then approached her car. "Tell her to hang in there. Dallas is gonna get its share of rain this week." She cocked her head at Lori in a questioning pose. "So you're back already?" Brittany remarked while pulling off her gardening gloves to examine her fancy manicure for chips. Today, her ever-changing nail design was an intricate, multihued Indian pattern in various shades of blue.

"It was a short run. No stop in Mexico City this time. Came straight through from Acapulco."

"How'd it go?" Brittany asked, now focusing on her neighbor instead of her nails.

"Really kinda strange."

"Strange? How?" Brittany asked.

"Well, there was this guy on the plane…. I danced with him

at a club in Acapulco the night before and this morning, there he was…on my flight! And he started coming on to me like crazy."

"You call that strange?" Brittany quipped. "Please. Call it good luck…that is if he's got it goin' on."

Lori grinned. "He had it goin' on all right."

"Good. So what happened? You gonna see him?"

"I dunno. I've gotta think this one through. I can't jump in too fast and have another situation, you know?"

"Uh-hmm," Brittany murmured in agreement. "After Devan… I do understand."

"Anyway, we left it at a handshake at the airport, but I do have his card," Lori replied, not quite ready to share her true feelings about her encounter with Ramón. Besides, she wasn't sure how she felt about him. She only knew that his kiss had shaken her up and awakened feelings she wanted to explore. The man's image was taking up residence in her head, and Lori was sure they'd meet again one day. She stretched her neck, tilted her head to one side and gave Brittany a choppy wave. "Gotta go…I'm exhausted."

"After you get some rest, come over for dinner. You remember Janice and Tom Evans—the newlyweds who just moved in over on Willow Trails?"

"Yeah, nice couple."

"Well, I invited them over for dinner yesterday. We barbecued. I've got plenty of leftover chicken and ribs."

"Umm, sounds great. Think I *will* take you up on that," Lori decided, pressing the remote to raise her garage door.

After parking her car, Lori grabbed her luggage and entered her house through the connecting door that led into the kitchen. Leaving her rolling bag by the entryway, she went to the back window and opened the plantation blinds to let some light into the room. Turning around, she reached for her bag, but stopped dead in her tracks, unable to believe her eyes.

"My God. What happened here?" she hissed under her breath, though a scream was rising fast in her throat. The sight that greeted Lori was shocking, terrifying. Her heart thumped in fear as she eyed the scene in terror.

Swirls of bright blue paint were splattered over every surface of the room. The glass tabletop was smeared with a childish finger-paint scrawl, as were the granite kitchen countertops, the stainless-steel refrigerator and the center butcher-block island. Even the imported Italian wall tiles that Lori had paid entirely too much for, were emblazoned with jagged symbols and lines that made no sense at all. Thinking that the vandals might still be in the house, she quickly stepped back, eager to get out of the house before she became their next victim.

On her way out, Lori brushed her arm against the paint-splattered doorjamb, but saw nothing on her skin. Turning around, she stepped deeper into the room and slid a trembling finger over the blue graffiti on the front of the refrigerator, realizing that the vandals must have done their thing some time ago because all their trashy artwork was bone dry. Because of that, she doubted that anyone was still there.

More angry than frightened, she ran toward the front of the house, stuck her head into her champagne-and-sage-hued bedroom and gaped at the bright yellow stripes painted down the middle of her satin, queen-size bedspread. Lumps of the same color paint had dripped onto the carpet and dried into lumpy pools that looked like ugly egg yolks. Stepping around the mess, she peeked into her master bath and cursed out loud. "Damn, damn, damn!" The glass in her antique oval mirror had been shattered. Shards of glass littered the vanity and the floor.

From the bedroom, Lori hurried to inspect the rest of the house, including closets and jewelry boxes and found that, luckily, there was no more damage and no valuables missing. Infuriated, she punched 911 into her cell phone and screamed at the operator who answered.

"I need the police! Right away! My home has been vandalized!" she shouted, unable to control the adrenalin pushing her emotions into overdrive.

"My address?" Lori gulped down her fear and centered her thoughts, forcing herself to focus. "Fifty-two-seventy-one Falls Trail Drive."

"The police are on the way. Are you hurt?" the operator wanted to know.

"No, I'm fine."

"Are you still inside the house?"

"Yes."

"Get out now."

"I've looked through the house. No one is here."

"Leave anyway. Go outside and wait for the police," the take-charge operator ordered. "Did you walk in on the vandals?"

"No, I just returned from a three-day trip to Mexico," Lori explained, exiting the bedroom. "I'm a flight attendant... I'm away a lot. Never had any trouble. I can't believe this..." She stopped abruptly, glanced back at her ruined kitchen, and then yanked the front door open and hurried across her driveway toward Brittany, who was still outside preening her rose bushes.

"What's the matter?" Brittany asked, seeing the terror on Lori's face. "Trouble at Globus? Who's on the phone?"

"The police."

"What?"

"Right. You won't believe this, Brit. Somebody vandalized my house. Everything...is covered...with...graffiti," Lori sputtered as she described the scene.

"Shit! You gotta be kidding," Brittany snapped. She threw her clippers to the ground and grabbed hold of Lori's arm. "Nobody's inside, right?"

"No, but it's a mess in there. Did you hear anything last night? See any suspicious-looking people hanging around?" Lori wanted to know.

"No. Nothing. As I said, Janice and Tom came over for dinner. We had the outdoor speakers turned up pretty loud while we were on the patio. They left about ten. Must have happened after I went inside. I didn't hear anything unusual." Brittany glanced back at Lori's house. "Did they kick in the back door? Break a window?"

"I don't know...I didn't look to see..." Lori stopped, turning around to focus on the black and white patrol car with whirling red and blue lights that swept up to the curb and jolted to a stop.

Pushing her cell phone into her uniform pocket, she approached the tall black man who unfolded his towering uniformed body from the squad car and hooked his thumbs into his holster belt. "Officer. Thanks for coming so quickly." Lori rushed to welcome the policeman.

"Detective Clint Washington," he told Lori, without extending his hand. He surveyed her house with inquisitive eyes, seemingly already on the case and primed for action. "What happened here?" he asked, listening as Lori described what she'd discovered on her return home.

"Let's check it out," he stated with calm authority, striding off. His long legs devoured Lori's brick-paved walkway in five giant steps, leaving Lori and Brittany to tag along behind.

Once inside, they went into the bedroom, and then checked the master bath. "We do have a few good fingerprints, here on the edge of the basin," he told Lori. "That's encouraging. I'll get the crime scene investigation team out here right away. You can go ahead and sweep up the broken glass, but don't touch the paint smears, okay?"

Lori nodded in relief, hoping the prints might help the police catch whoever did this.

"Are you sure nothing of value was stolen?" Washington asked after he'd inspected the rest of the damage and determined that the vandals had cut the wires to Lori's alarm box and broken a window in the dining room to get into the house.

"Certain. Nothing is missing, I checked everywhere I could think of," Lori assured him. She watched him open a pad of forms and begin to fill one out.

"So this was for kicks?" Brittany snapped in disgust. "I can't believe some damn sicko would do this just for fun." Brittany directed her anger toward Detective Washington, whose shoulders leveled off at the top of the petite woman's head. "That is some crazy shit, you know?" she blurted out.

Lori cut her eyes at her friend, warning her about her language. Back in the day, Brittany's startling potty mouth might have been a ratings winner when she was playing a rebellious teenager on a television sitcom, but that kind of language was definitely out of place when dealing with the police.

"Oh, excuse my language, detective," Brittany muttered. "But I'm sure you know what I mean."

"Unfortunately, I do," the policeman agreed, turning intensely serious eyes on Brittany. "This kind of vandalism happens all the time. It's June. School just let out. Kids with too much time and too little to do wind up pulling stunts like this for kicks. Just last week, two streets over, we had the same kind of thing—only red paint that time."

"So what are the police doing about it?" Lori demanded, fear now shifting into outrage. "Can't you catch the punks who are ruining the subdivision before they strike again?"

"You're just one of many on my watch. The kids will slip up, and we'll catch 'em, but in the meantime, keep your eyes open for any suspicious activity. Might want to get a dog. A barking dog does a good job of scaring prowlers off."

"A dog?" Lori rolled her eyes and pressed a finger to the company name embroidered on her blouse. "As you can see, I'm employed by Globus-Americas. I travel all the time. No way can I take on the responsibility of a dog."

"Well, then, a more effective alarm system might help," the detective suggested, handing Lori the police report to sign.

With a sigh, Lori signed the paper, took her copy and then escorted the officer out. As she watched him drive away, she felt discouraged and very uneasy. "I doubt the police will ever catch the punks who wrecked my house," she said to Brittany as they turned and walked up the driveway.

"He sure was fine," Brittany murmured, ignoring Lori's comment.

"Fine?" Lori's head whipped around. "What are you talking about?"

"Detective Washington. Big feet, long legs. A killer smile. Umm, he's got it all going on."

Lori punched Brittany on the shoulder. "Get outta here! You're checking out the brother when we need to be pushing him to do his job? Brittany Adams, you need to quit."

"Hey, my radar is always on, and he was one good-looking black dot on my screen. He's obviously well employed and wasn't wearing any rings."

"Girl, please," Lori sighed in frustration. "The last time you got involved with a policeman, you wound up chasing the guy out of your house with a pot of hot coffee in one hand and a kitchen knife in the other."

"Nat Chavis was FBI, not local," Brittany defended. "And it was a mug of hot coffee, not a pot."

"Whatever," Lori quipped. "All I remember is that he treated you like a suspect and you snapped when you found out he'd bugged your cell phone."

"Nat was a fool…he underestimated my intelligence," Brittany said calmly, chin raised. "But this Detective Washington, now, he looks like a man with good sense."

Lori paused at her front door and pinned her neighbor with a warning expression. "Let's just hope he uses his good sense to get the fools who trashed my house."

Brittany came up beside Lori, nodding. "But…as the handsome, intelligent, hopefully single detective said, one police car can't be everywhere all the time. If thieves and vandals want to get in, they'll find a way."

"Yeah." Lori grimaced in agreement. "I get the impression that we're kinda on our own."

Brittany grunted. "Well, I'm not gonna put bars on my windows and doors to keep some punk-ass kids from spray painting my living room, and I refuse like hell to buy a gun. Just my luck I'd wind up shooting the mail carrier in the ass."

"Unfortunately, it all comes down to making it hard for someone to get in," Lori observed, her mind turning back to what the officer had said. *What you need is a better alarm system.*

"Brit, I gotta go," Lori quipped, giving her neighbor a quick wave goodbye.

"Need any help cleaning up?"

"Naw. I'll sweep up the glass, but I'll have to leave everything else until the crime scene investigators are finished. I'll be over later. Save me some ribs."

Inside her house, Lori reached into her skirt pocket, removed Ramón's business card and stared at it, her heart lurching in her chest at the thought of hearing his voice and seeing him again. She picked up the phone, pressed in two numbers, but then stopped.

"I'll call first thing in the morning," she decided, not yet ready to trust her voice. Not ready to betray her feelings for a man who was quickly winding his way into her heart.

## Chapter 6

Ramón slid the bacon and spinach omelet he'd just made onto a plate and sat down at the breakfast table in his condo. It was only seven-thirty in the morning, but he had already completed his daily three-mile run, showered and was looking forward to breakfast. Ramón wasn't much of a cook, but he could put together a hell of an omelet. Since he watched his diet carefully, he ate a light lunch and dinner was most often a steak and fresh vegetables at the Big Tex Steak House two blocks from his house.

With a flick of his thumb, he scrolled through messages on his cell phone while eating, replying to those that required a response, deleting a bunch of spam. The three days he'd spent in Acapulco with his brother had put him behind schedule, but now that he was back in Houston, it was time to get on track and back to work.

After he finished reading and responding to his e-mails he shifted his focus to the workday ahead. He had two commercial estimates to prepare, a whole-house installation to inspect and equipment to pick up at the electrical supply house. But before he did any of that he wanted to drop by the assisted living center and say hello to his dad.

While plotting his day, his cell phone rang and he quickly recognized Lori's name and number.

"Vida-Shield Security," he said, using his business greeting and tamping down his excitement over the fact that she was calling.

"Ramón Vidal, please," Lori said.

"This is Ramón."

"Oh, great. This is Lori Myles...from the airplane. Remember me?"

"Of course. How could I forget?" Ramón responded, intentionally lowering his voice in an attempt to sound relaxed and calm. "Glad you called. Wasn't sure you would."

"Well, before you get too excited... I have to tell you, this is not a social call. I need your help."

Ramón squinted at the sliding-glass door leading onto his patio, where hanging baskets of ivy and ferns created a lush, quiet retreat. He considered her remark and decided that it was better to be needed than ignored. At least she'd turned to *him*. "Okay...shoot. What can I do for you?" he offered as casually as possible, thrilled that she wanted his input on whatever was on her mind.

"I'm not sure where to start. I'm still so angry I can hardly talk about what happened."

Ramón's initial pleasure at hearing from Lori quickly shifted to alarm. She sounded so intense. So frightened. And so different from when they'd chatted on the plane. Something terrible must have happened. "What's going on?" he asked, listening as she described the scene that greeted her when she arrived home. He got up from the table and began to pace his kitchen, frowning at the floor, disturbed by what she was telling him.

"All right. I know you're upset, but try to calm down," he encouraged, sensing how nervous she was. During the flight to Houston, she had been the epitome of calm, a poised professional woman who was totally in control of her emotions, but now she was rattling on in a nervous sputter that sent off bells of alarm.

"Are *you* okay?" he wanted to know when she finally paused to catch her breath.

"I'm fine," Lori assured Ramón.

"Where'd you sleep last night?"

"Next door…at my neighbor's house."

"Good. How do you feel today?"

"Shaken up and mad as hell. I don't understand why my burglar alarm didn't alert the police when the vandals broke in."

"Do you have a wireless alarm?" Ramón inquired.

"Yes, I think so," Lori replied.

"That means your keypad, circuit board, backup battery and siren were most likely all in one unit," Ramón added.

"Yeah, probably so. It came with the house, so I never paid much attention to what kind of system I had," Lori said.

"Well, the burglars could have completely disabled your unit before it had time to send a signal to the police."

"Really?"

"Yeah," Ramón confirmed. "Happens all the time."

"The detective who came out to take the report was nice," Lori added. "But he wasn't very encouraging. He said there've been a few incidents like mine since school let out. Local kids who are bored, he thinks."

"Yeah, sounds like that," Ramón agreed. "But that doesn't make them any less dangerous than hard-core criminals. If I were you, I'd take this seriously."

"I plan to. That's why I called. The vandals destroyed my system. Smashed the control box and stripped all the wires. Think you can you fix it?"

"I can try, but if you have an all-in-one unit, I'd replace it. They're extremely vulnerable and create a false sense of security. What you need is a hardwired cellular system that communicates an alarm signal in less than thirty seconds. Let me take a look at what you have and we can go from there. I can come over this morning, if you want," Ramón offered, surprised by how easily he was agreeing to rearrange his schedule and how much he already cared about Lori.

"Would you?" Lori asked.

"Of course."

"Great. The crime scene investigators were here at daybreak. They got what they needed and left. Now I need to find someone to deal with all this paint," she went on, voice raw with indecision. "This mess is gonna require a lot more than a mop and a broom. Paint is everywhere. My mirrors are shattered. The carpet is ruined. I can't... I don't..."

When Lori's voice cracked and the phone went silent, Ramón flinched, stung by Lori's frustration, as well as her shock over what had happened. He'd been in the home security business long enough to sense how she was feeling right now. She was hurt, stunned and confused about what to do.

"First thing you need to do is call your insurance company," he offered.

"I did. They're sending someone out today," Lori said.

"Good. I can give you the name of a restoration company I've used. They do a good job and accept whatever insurance pays."

"That would help a lot," Lori replied, clearly relieved.

"Be sure to take pictures before the cleaning service deals with the paint, too," he added.

Having been inside vandalized homes more than a few times, Ramón could visualize the scene: precious treasures trashed, carefully appointed décor ruined. In an instant, everything that had once been clean and shiny was now dirty and ugly, sullied by an intruder's touch. The emotional toll that such an incident took could be very heavy.

"Okay, I'll bring some plywood to board up your broken window," he told Lori, wanting to do whatever he could to ease her anxiety. No way was he going to let her go through this alone.

"What's your address?" he asked, grabbing a pen to scribble the street name and number on the back of a dry-cleaning receipt as he calculated how far away she lived. "Hold it together, okay? I've got a quick stop to make and then I'll call you when I'm nearby."

\* \* \*

Tomás Vidal wiped a tear from his eye and then looked at Ramón, who was seated beside him in the recreation room of the assisted living center. "What a wonderful thing to witness," Tomás whispered in a quiet tone. "My boy is now a federal judge. Amazing, but not surprising. He worked hard to make it, you know? I remember when your mother and I left Mexico and came to Texas. Xavier was just a boy. And now he's a big-shot judge. I only wish your mother could have lived to see this day."

Ramón closed the DVD player they had been viewing, set it on the coffee table and looked at his father, his mind suddenly turning back to the days they had spent together deep-sea fishing in the Gulf. Setting out before dawn, looking forward to a day at sea and a huge catch to bring home had been wonderful. But those days were gone forever. Never again would he go fishing with his father, whose health was deteriorating very quickly. It pained Ramón to see Tomás Vidal withering into a shell of a man right before his eyes. His father's thick black hair was now nearly all gray, his once bright eyes no longer shone with the gleam of life that Ramón remembered and the skin around his thin lips was more puckered with tiny wrinkles than Ramón had seen on his last visit. With each passing day, Ramón knew his time with his father was getting shorter, so he wanted to make each moment they spent together count. Bringing along the DVD of Xavier's swearing-in ceremony had brightened Tomás's day and given him much to discuss with his fellow residents at the assisted living center.

"Pop," Ramón began. "I know Mom is up in Heaven watching us right now and she knows what's going on."

Tomás laughed and winked at his son. "She always knew what was going on with you two boys. Not much escaped her, you know?"

"For real," Ramón replied. "She was on my case every day."

"That's why you and Xavier turned out to be such fine young men. Because your mother taught you how to appreciate what you have and how to make the most of the talent God gave you."

"I've tried to make you proud, Pop."

"And you have," Tomás agreed, reaching out to take hold of Ramón's hand. "But there is one thing I want you to do, Ramón. Time is moving on, son. You need to do what your brother has done. Get married and start a family so I can enjoy more grandchildren before I leave this world."

Tilting his head back, Ramón let his father's words sink in, realizing how true they were. He gave his father's hand a firm squeeze, and said, "I'm working on that one, Pop. Just be patient, okay?"

When Ramón walked into Lori's house, he did a double take and then smiled. The last time he'd seen her she had been dressed in her GAA uniform, looking spiffy and totally in charge. Now she was wearing black stretch pants, thong sandals and a skimpy white halter top that showed off smooth tan shoulders and a lot more cleavage than he had seen on the dance floor. She looked like a teenager with her hair, now freed from its neat French twist, falling loosely around her face in a soft cascade of jet-black curls that brushed cheeks devoid of makeup.

Lori propped her broom against the table in the foyer and grinned at Ramón, sending a jolt of pleasure straight into his gut.

"Hi," she said, wiping her brow with the back of one hand. "You just called! Either you were already close by or you broke the speed limit getting here. Which is it?"

"I wasn't that far away. Stopped to see my dad."

"Really? Where does he live?"

"Old Mill Assisted Living Center."

"Oh, yeah. Over on Huffman near Broad?"

"Right. After I left him, I headed straight here. And yes, I did keep an eye on my rearview mirror for any black and whites that might be on my tail," he said with a wink, knowing he'd rolled through that last stop sign at the intersection leading to Lori's street—after looking both ways, of course.

During the drive to her house, he'd thought of nothing but how shaky her voice had sounded on the phone, how anxious and panicky she must be. He was not about to leave her house

until he had done all he could to make her feel safe. "Give that
to me," he told Lori, taking hold of the broom. "Go sit down and
watch TV or something. Let me take over from here."

"Oh, no you don't," she said forcefully, tugging on the
broomstick, her eyes squinting in earnest. "Sweeping up glass,
I can do. Fixing a trashed alarm? No. So you get busy with the
alarm, while I clean up the rest of this glass."

"You've got a deal. Show me where the control box is and
leave it to me," Ramón agreed.

"It's in the garage. And it's stifling hot out there. I can hook
up a fan if you want."

"No, I'll be fine," Ramón commented, following Lori through
the kitchen toward the door to the garage. However, walking
behind her, what he really wanted was to place both palms on her
sweet round hips, which were so deliciously encased in her black
Capri pants. The sight was too beautiful for words. Sucking in a
breath, he ripped his eyes away from her perfectly shaped rear
end. The last thing he wanted was for Lori to turn around and
see the growing bulge in his pants, though he knew there was
no way to slow his growing desire to possess her completely.


Once Lori restored as much order to her trashed bedroom as
possible, she stripped her bed of ruined linens, stuffed them in
two heavy-duty trash bags and headed through the kitchen to
the garage. There she paused in the doorway and drank in the
delicious sight of Ramón, shirtless, standing in the garage with
his back to her while removing the broken control box.

Lori's heart did a jerky flip, sending pulses of heat between
her legs and into the pit of her stomach. He looked so damn good
with his longish black hair tied back with a red handkerchief and
his smooth V-shaped torso glistening back at her. Lori ran her
tongue over her bottom lip and gulped back the surprising surge
of desire that rose within her. As she watched him twist wires
and adjust levers, she realized that he was singing the song they
had danced to in Club Azule. Was that a coincidence, or was he
trying to send her some kind of a message?

*Damn he's hot! Why did he have to take off his shirt? Show me so much skin? Tempt me like this when the last thing I need is to get tangled up with a stranger?*

"There's a radio over there on that shelf," she said casually, stepping into the garage.

Ramón's head swiveled around in surprise. He flashed a killer smile at her, sending more pulses of heat through Lori, who drew in a short breath to cool down. After depositing the trash bags in the large rolling bin, she went over to the cluttered shelf, picked up a battered boom box and handed it to Ramón. "Here. Put it on any station you want. Then you won't have to sing to yourself."

Ramón reached out, as if to take the radio, but covered her hand with his instead. With an insistent tug, he guided her closer, slipped his hands beneath her arms and cupped her elbows with his palms. Only the small blue radio that Lori was holding prevented her body from molding flush to his. "No, thanks," he replied in a husky tone. "I'd rather listen to my own singing… unless it rattles you."

His remark slid over Lori like a layer of sweet syrup, easing through her veins to pool in her chest. He had a way of saying the most mundane things in the most sensual way, stirring up emotions that threatened Lori's composure.

"Don't worry. You could never rattle me, unless I allowed you to," she countered, setting the radio down, shifting her hips to one side while eyeing Ramón with a dare of a gaze.

"Never?" he repeated. "You sound awfully sure about that."

"I am."

"Hmm. Okay. Let's give it a test. Does this rattle you?" he whispered, feathering a finger along the side of her neck and down to rest on her bare shoulder.

"Not at all," Lori replied, luxuriating in the shivers initiated by his touch, knowing it was pointless to deny that she was getting all hot and bothered. "In fact, that feels pretty good," she admitted, knowing she was telling the truth.

Encouraged, Ramón graced her with a misty half smile and then dipped down to graze his lips across hers in a brush of a kiss before pulling back to check her reaction. "How about that?"

Lori felt the muscles in her tunnel of love contract, relax and then tighten again as she connected with the yearning expression darkening his features.

"Getting close," she admitted, watching him with guarded eyes as his self-assured smile widened, brightening his face.

With just a touch on her cheek and a light brush of a kiss, he'd turned on the kind of sexual heat that Lori knew spelled trouble. There was no denying that his effect on her was too dramatic to ignore, too delicious to dismiss and too intensely inviting to pass up. However, she planned to keep a tight rein on the pace of this rapidly evolving encounter and not get caught up in the drama of too much togetherness too soon. Yes, Ramón did rattle her, but she liked the feeling of not knowing what to expect. He made her want to do things she shouldn't even be thinking about, let alone hoping would happen.

Ramón's heart was racing like a video on fast forward. In front of him stood the most beautiful and exciting woman he'd met in a long time, with her gorgeous face, vibrant energy and a teasing attitude that turned him on. He flattened his palms on the backs of her arms and inhaled her scent—delicate, sweet and as intoxicating as deep red wine. God, how he'd love to ease her down on the concrete garage floor and take her this very minute, and from the signals she was sending out, she just might be down with such a move.

During his drive to her house, he'd thought of the delicious press of her thighs on his, the warmth of her breasts filling his hands, the touch of her fingers on the erection that was now swelling in his pants. Now with tentative steps, Ramón guided Lori to the side of her car and positioned her back against the driver's-side door. He leaned over her, inching closer until the buds of her hardened nipples burned twin spots of desire into his bare chest. Bracing his hands against the car on either side of Lori's face, he locked her in place and studied her features with languorous eyes, not about to rush her into anything, though he sure as hell wasn't going to let an opportunity like this pass him by.

\* \* \*

Lori stilled under Ramón's piercing, dreamy brown eyes, knowing he was waiting for a go-ahead signal from her. Her body was taut, aching for his touch—and she didn't want the feeling to slip away. What she wanted was to feel him all over her, inside her, tasting and teasing and probing places that were in desperate need of attention.

*What the hell? How far can things go inside my garage?* she rationalized, arching forward and flattening her breasts against his chest while stifling the moan of joy that crept into her throat. She let him push her back against the car, inviting Ramón to press closer and devour her mouth in a deep, probing kiss. As their tongues explored and flicked over each other in their search for satisfaction, Ramón's fingers worked on the knot in the straps that held Lori's halter top in place. When the soft white fabric fell to her waist, Lori gulped back her need, parted her legs and guided Ramón to stand between them.

Lowering his head, he lifted one warm breast to his mouth and slid his tongue across the nipple before suckling it with a pull that ignited emotional flames in Lori. She welcomed the burn of his tongue and the scorch of his fingers, loving the blistering press of his pleasure-tool as it grew hard against the flat of her stomach.

"Hey, Lori!" Brittany's voice bounced against the closed garage door and jolted Lori out of her self-indulgent trance. "Ohmigod! It's my neighbor," Lori hissed, forcing Ramón to back away so she could pull up her halter top and re-tie the straps.

"Not a word," she whispered to Ramón as she pressed the button to raise the garage door, pushing an explosion of black curls out of her eyes.

"Hey, there you are," Brittany said, walking into the garage, her focus shifting from Lori to Ramón and then back to her neighbor. "No answer at the front door, so I thought you might be out here."

"Right, right. Just emptying the trash. Come on through," Lori rushed to say, beckoning Brittany forward. "Brittany, uh, this is Ramón Vidal…from Vida-Shield Security. He's fixing my alarm."

"Oh, yeah. I saw his truck in the driveway. Hello, Ramón," Brittany said with a nod in his direction. "Good idea to get that thing back up and running right away." She turned back to Lori. "Need any help cleaning up over here?"

"Thanks, but I think we've got it covered," Lori huffed, throwing a nervous glance at Ramón, who nodded his agreement and said, "Yeah, we're doing just fine."

Lori cringed at the hint of a smirk that tugged the corner of Ramón's mouth and the sexy tone he'd used, certain that Brittany must be wondering what was going on.

"Ramón is gonna fix the broken window in the dining room, too," Lori rushed to say. "And he's arranged for a cleaning company to come out and deal with the paint."

"You two are moving right along, huh?" Brittany observed.

"That's right," Ramón replied, reaching for his screwdriver and resuming his work. "Best to move quickly when you have a lot of ground to cover. Won't take me long to make Lori safe again."

"That'll be a relief," Lori remarked with a fast roll of her eyes at Ramón while making her way toward the door leading into the house. "Come on in, Brit. I can use a glass of water."

"Me, too," Brittany concurred, fanning her fingers in front of her face. "It's too damn hot to stay out here."

As soon as they were in the kitchen, Lori closed the door and leaned against it, her attention sharply focused on Brittany. "Okay… I know you didn't come over here just to offer your help or get a glass of water, did you?"

"Hell, no. When I saw Mr. Security Expert get out of his truck, I knew I had to see this guy up close. Is he for real? Shit…where'd you find a hunk like that to fix your alarm system?" she asked, stabbing Lori with a skeptical expression. "The Yellow Pages or a personal hookup?"

Adopting an amused, but pensive expression, Lori paused, and then said, "Personal connection."

"Okaaaay…so, he's a friend?"

"I guess you could call him that," Lori hedged, removing two glasses from the cabinet, which she filled with ice and cold water from her refrigerator door.

Brittany tapped a long acrylic fingernail on Lori's kitchen counter, signaling her curiosity. "He's a new friend, then? One I have neither seen nor heard of before today, and one who is hellafine."

"On that we do agree." Lori laughed conspiratorially.

"When did you meet him? Where?" Brittany demanded, accepting her drink from Lori.

"He's the guy I told you about…the one I met on the plane yesterday. Well, no…before that when I danced with him in the club in Acapulco," she finished in a stammer of words.

A burst of laughter made Brittany step back. "When you said he had it goin' on, you really meant it."

Lori locked wide innocent eyes on Brittany. "Did I say that?"

"You did."

"Yeah, well, what's your take?" Lori probed.

"I'm not saying anything," Brittany shot back. "Just observing, and from the looks on your two faces when I walked into the garage, I'd say he's in more trouble than you." Chuckling, Brittany sipped her water, and then jerked her head toward the closed garage door. "Come on, let's go back out there. I want to see more of your gorgeous new friend. In fact, I have a few questions for him."

Back in the garage, Ramón had bad news. "Sorry to tell you, Lori, but your system is not worth repairing."

Lori grimaced, shoulders sagging down in disappointment. "Damn. What do you suggest?"

"A whole new system," he stated in a serious tone, going on to describe his most popular home security alarm. "It has a multilevel digital alarm that's virtually tamperproof. I can take the measurements today, plan it out for you and install it tomorrow if you want."

"Well, I guess so. Think insurance will pay?"

"I'm sure they will. If you give me your agent's name, I'll verify everything before I proceed," Ramón offered, clearly enjoying the fact that he could be of help.

"Okay, I'll get his member," Lori said, turning to go inside.

"Ramón," Brittany started as soon as Lori had left the garage, "What's your opinion of burglar bars?"

"Not always a good idea," he said, kneeling to put his tools into his toolbox.

Brittany walked up behind Ramón and stared at his bare back, shaking her head in admiration while mouthing the words, *Too damn fine!* "Why not burglar bars?" she asked.

Ramón stopped what he was doing and looked up at Brittany. "Well, they could cause more harm than good," he said, sounding like an authority. "If you get trapped inside a house with those bars when you need to get out, you're doomed. If you decide to install them, just make sure they have release latches on the inside."

"Makes sense," Brittany replied, unable to tear her eyes off Ramón when he stood up and pulled his T-shirt over his head, just as Lori retuned with the insurance agent's number.

"Thanks," he said, appraising Lori with obvious longing. "Tomorrow, I'll install an entirely new system. There are several models to choose from. If you want…"

"Whatever you recommend," Lori interrupted, confident that he would not steer her wrong.

"As long as it keeps those punk-ass vandals out," Brittany spoke up. "Summer vacation has only just started. Who knows how bad this might get over the summer? We all gotta be prepared."

"You might want to think about starting a community-watch program out here," Ramón suggested, snapping on his red baseball cap.

"Humm. How's that work? Are the police involved?" Brittany wanted to know.

"Oh, yeah. They partner with citizens' watch programs all the time. They'll help you organize patrols, provide training and serve as backup when you need them."

"That sounds like a good, proactive approach. What would we have to do?" Lori inquired, intrigued by the idea of taking an active role in protecting herself.

"You just get the residents together and form teams to walk

or drive the streets. You'll send a message to the criminals that you're not gonna sit back and let them take control of your neighborhood," Ramón replied, going on to tell Brittany and Lori about other subdivisions in the area that had decreased crime substantially after starting such a program. "Act now and you put the punks on notice."

Lori gestured toward Ramón, head slanted to the side. "Think you could come and demonstrate your ultrasafe home security systems at our next homeowners' meeting?"

"Be happy to," Ramón replied, tossing a spool of duct tape into his toolbox. "I'm at your disposal. All you have to do is tell me what you want."

Lori blinked, tamped down a smile and exhaled a soft breath.

"Aaall right…" Brittany said, filling the awkward lull in a too loud voice. "Where do we start?"

"Call your homeowners' association president and suggest a meeting with a rep from the police department who could come out and explain what's involved," Ramón offered.

"Well, Detective Washington was very nice. Maybe we should ask him to be our liaison," Brittany volunteered.

"I'm sure you'd like that," Lori agreed with a You're-not-fooling-anybody look.

"He knows our situation and knows what's going on," Brittany said.

"Why don't *you* give him a call?" Lori suggested.

"I will. I'll call him right now and see if he'll agree to help us," Brittany said. With a choppy finger wave, she hurried down the driveway and across her lawn to disappear inside her house.

As soon as Brittany left, Lori lowered the garage door and turned to face Ramón. "Come on, I'll show you where the broken window is."

Without a word, Ramón reached out and slipped his index finger under the strap of Lori's halter top. "Or we could pick up where we were before your neighbor interrupted."

Lori hesitated for a nanosecond, seriously considering his proposal, but knew better than to act on her out-of-control desires. She quickly removed his hand from her halter top strap and said,

"No way. We have too much to do. We can't be messing around like this anymore."

Lori pivoted around and started to walk away.

Ramón stopped her with a hand on her arm. "Why can't we do both?" he softly urged, voice rough and low.

"Because well, we just can't," Lori stuttered, flustered by the beam of lust he was shooting at her in a seductive squint that was impossible to ignore. Now that she'd allowed him to sample her private treasures, he clearly wanted more. And she did, too.

## Chapter 7

The blare of hard-core heavy-metal music jerked Lori out of her dream.

*Damn! I was just getting into that scene,* she grumbled, reaching over to smash the Off button on her clock-radio alarm. Six o'clock. Time to get up. *But not just yet,* she decided, rolling onto her back to snuggle deeper into her pillow. How disappointing! Ramón was not lying in bed beside her with his lips nibbling her ear while his hands roamed her body. Awakening so abruptly had left Lori frustrated, sexually aroused and wishing her dream had not ended. She sighed aloud, seriously contemplating calling Ramón just to hear his voice.

*Would he be awake this early?* she wondered, trying to imagine what he was doing and how would he react if she called. Probably think she was horny as hell. *And I am,* she decided with a chuckle. How long had it been since she'd felt this taken by a man? *Obviously, long enough to seriously consider making the first move,* she concluded, shaking off the aftermath of her dream to sit up and lean against the headboard.

There was still a lot to do in the house, even though yesterday's cleaning crew had used vacuums, paint removers and solvents to restore her countertops and floors to their former pristine condition. She wrinkled her nose at the lingering scent of paint, thankful that her insurance would cover all the repairs.

She glanced into her master bath to look at the new mirrors Ramón had installed.

"Pretty handy guy to have around," she observed, swinging her legs over the side of the bed. In a few hours he'd be back to replace her alarm system. She could hardly wait to see him.

After a quick shower, a cup of coffee and a slice of melon, Lori was loading the dishwasher when the telephone rang. Reaching for the handset, she checked the screen and confirmed her suspicion: Trish Myles's name was flashing in big letters.

"Hi, Mom," Lori greeted in as enthusiastic a voice as she could muster so early in the day. Though her divorced mother lived in Dallas, which was either a one-hour flight or a four-hour drive from Houston, Lori didn't make the trip often enough to suit her mother. Since holidays were peak travel time, Lori usually worked on the days that most families spent together, leaving her mother to celebrate with close friends and neighbors instead of her only child.

"You're up early," Lori commented.

"If I don't call early, I usually can't get to you," Trish complained to her daughter, sounding deadly serious. "You're always flitting off here or there. Never know where you are or if you're okay. You have time to go everywhere except to visit me. Anyway, I'm glad I caught you today."

Lori let her mother's gentle criticism pass. They engaged in this same dance of words every time they spoke. Their personalities were so different that Lori used to wonder if she'd been adopted. "Well, I do have a cell phone, you know. You can call me anytime."

"And try to have a conversation with you while you're running through the airport or on the runway preparing to take off?" Trish huffed. "No, I'd rather wait and catch you at home, when you don't have so much on your mind."

*If you only knew what's on my mind today,* Lori thought with a sigh, going on to tell her mother, "I'm on a little bit of a break right now…just got back from Acapulco. It's great to finally have a regular schedule. I promise to come for a visit. Soon."

"I'd like that. You should see my rose garden. It was slow taking off, but now every bush is in full bloom. My Golden Lady is doing so well. Try to come before the weather gets too hot and everything starts to fade."

"I will," Lori promised, knowing how much her mother loved showing off her roses. When Lori was growing up, she spent many hours with her mother, planting, pruning and spraying the thorny plants that erupted in a blaze of color all over their backyard. For her eighth birthday, Lori's mother had given her a Precious Pink rose to nurture, and Lori had won first prize for her miniature pink blooms after entering it into an exhibit at the Dallas County Fair. Memories of those days spent working beside her mother in the garden were some of Lori's fondest, because as Lori grew into an independent woman, it seemed as if her relationship with her mother became more and more difficult to manage.

"Sometimes I wish you were still working reserve," Trish observed, jerking Lori back to their conversation. "You had so much more free time then…"

"Well, things have changed," Lori interrupted to remind her mother. "I'm a lineholder now and don't ever plan to go back on reserve." A stilted pause followed, allowing Lori to mentally count to ten in order not to say something she might regret.

By now her mother, who did not fly and had never wanted Lori to become a flight attendant, ought to understand the nature of her job. In the airline industry, seniority determined a flight attendant's status as either a lineholder or a reserve. Lineholders had their flying schedules set at least one month in advance, while reserves filled open flying time and covered positions vacated by senior crew members who called in sick or went on vacation. Lori had worked reserve for four long years before snagging an assignment on the coveted Houston/Mexico City/Acapulco route, and had no intentions of ever working reserve again.

"So what's going on with you besides your rose garden?" Lori inquired, changing the subject.

"I called to tell you about my trip to D.C.," Trish replied.

"Oh, right. Have a good time?" Lori asked, listening as her mother described in detail the museums, monuments, restaurants and sights that she and her travel club had visited while touring the capital city.

At fifty-two, Trish Myles was an attractive woman in good health who loved her job as principal of the elementary school that Lori had attended as a child. A conservative, cautious person, Trish prided herself on taking as few risks as possible, and did not understand how her only daughter had turned out to have such wanderlust, possessing what she considered to be a dangerously adventuresome soul.

Since divorcing Lori's father five years ago, Trish Myles took trips with a group from her church—but only by motor coach—to various parts of the country. Her most recent excursion had been to the nation's capital.

"It was… Well, all I can say is, it was not what I expected," Trish was saying. "Our tour guide was brand-new. Only on the job four days! I think the people on the tour knew more about the city than he did. And…to top it off, we had a terrible time on the way home."

"What happened?" Lori inquired, her stomach sinking, wishing her mother didn't have to find fault with every aspect of anything she did. They were so different. A veteran traveler, Lori had learned long ago to roll with the punches, to find something pleasurable in the most difficult of circumstances. After all, travel should be approached as an adventure, an exploration of the unknown, and you had to be prepared for whatever came along.

"The bus broke down outside New Orleans," Trish continued. "We spent the night in an awful motel. Dingy sheets, lukewarm showers and no cable or even pay-per-view movies. And guess what else?"

"What?" Lori asked, curious about how far her mother planned to go in her criticism of the trip.

"Road Runner Transit refused to pay for our rooms."

Lori bit back a smart retort, not surprised by the news. "Didn't I warn you not to go with them?" Lori said. Her online research had revealed many negative customer reviews.

"I know the company had a few complaints, but we saved so much money by choosing them," Trish defended.

"Money saved doesn't mean much if you're inconvenienced during your trip and stressed out when you arrive at your destination. Shoulda flown GAA."

"Lori, you know I don't fly—never will—and neither do any of the club members. Things can go wrong on airplanes, too, you know."

"I guess you're right," Lori conceded, ending the banter on this same old discussion. Lori wished her mother could be more flexible. Maybe years of corralling unruly children through the halls of Westwood Elementary School had made her mom so rigid and dead-set on order that it was difficult to change.

"What are you doing today?" Trish asked.

"Well, something happened here at the house," Lori reluctantly revealed, wishing she didn't have to tell her mom about the break-in. But she knew there was no getting around it. "My house was vandalized while I was away."

"That sounds scary," Trish said, listening as Lori described the damage. "Vandals are breaking in like that up here in Dallas, too. They just kick in doors and take what they want. You want me to come and stay with you for a while? I could drive down today and…"

"No, Mom. I'm fine. Everything's under control. The police are on the case. I'm getting a new alarm system today." The last thing Lori wanted was for her mother to jump in her Dodge minivan and rush to Houston to make sure her only daughter—a full-grown adult woman who flew around the world for a living—was safe. Not that she wouldn't like to see her mom, but Ramón was due any minute. Total privacy was what Lori craved. With her body and mind still primed for sex after her interrupted dream, Lori knew anything could happen. But was she prepared to satiate the cascade of raw need that Ramón had sparked only two days ago? As much as she tried to deny it, Lori knew she wanted to try.

# Chapter 8

When Ramón arrived, he was all business and got right to work on Lori's new alarm system. He didn't flirt with her or even act as if he'd nearly pulled her down on the garage floor and made love to her the day before. Not sure if she was pleased or irked by his new attitude, Lori decided to leave Ramón alone to complete the job he'd come to do while she went shopping.

By the time she retuned home with three Macy's shopping bags and five sacks of groceries, Ramón had finished installing her system, which he demonstrated with pride.

"It's not wise to think that the sound of an alarm will protect your home and yourself," Ramón explained as he showed Lori how to operate her new protective device. "Your old setup left you vulnerable. However, your hardwired alarm is now linked to a central station that receives signals from your alarm, checks the signal's authenticity and then notifies the appropriate law enforcement authorities right away. You also have fire and heat detection devices, so if a temperature gauge goes into alarm mode, your monitors will dispatch the fire department immediately."

Lori nodded her approval. "So hardwired is better than

wireless, huh?" she clarified, trying to grasp all the details that Ramón was tossing at her.

"Absolutely, a hardwired home alarm system cannot be easily compromised, even by a seasoned burglar. Ripping the keypad off the wall won't prevent this system from issuing an alarm, and it won't keep the alarm from sending its signal, either. It's even operational during a power failure."

"Fantastic. Now, what's the connection to my phone line?"

"The phone jack enables your alarm to 'seize' the phone line to send its signal to the monitoring center. So if a burglar takes your phone off the hook, your alarm will still be able to communicate with the outside world."

"Wow," Lori replied, impressed that Ramón had gone to such lengths to make sure she was well protected, and grateful for his attention to every detail of the installation.

"Your house is virtually burglarproof now," he said, packing up his tools and preparing to leave.

When he snapped the lid of his toolbox shut and tossed his toolbelt over his shoulder, Lori experienced a jolt of alarm. She didn't want him to go. In fact, she hadn't appreciated his cool, hands-off attitude, even though she'd insisted that he back off. It was six o'clock—time for dinner—and Lori did not want to eat alone.

"Why don't you stay and have dinner with me?" Lori blurted out. "You worked hard all day and I doubt you made any dinner plans. Did you?" What she didn't say was that they had hardly seen each other all day and she desperately wanted some alone time with him.

"Stay for dinner?" Ramón repeated. "Are you kidding? Of course, I will. You've got yourself a deal." He hefted his toolbox and pulled on his cap. "But only on one condition," he added.

"What's that?" Lori asked.

"You let me use your shower to clean up."

Lori gave him a skeptical look. "A shower? Well, sure, I guess. But, do you have clean clothes?"

"Hey, I always keep a change of clothes in a bag in my truck. Never know when I have to go from installing an outdoor system to meeting a prospective client. I like to be prepared for anything."

"I see," she murmured, a sly smile creeping over her lips as she imagined his naked body in her shower, water sluicing over those hard, washboard abs, trickling down the curves of his tight, round butt and into the sudsy patch of hair at the base of his... She gave herself a mental jolt and blinked at Ramón. "A shower. Sure, then you'll stay for dinner?"

"Damn straight," Ramón agreed.

"Good," Lori replied. "Go get your bag and I'll get you some towels."

Heading into her master bath, she removed a set of fresh linens from the closet and set them on the counter, pausing to fantasize about joining him under the spray of the jets to rub delicious-smelling shower gel all over his back. Hmm...did she dare go that far? Turning to leave, she came face-to-face with Ramón, whose eyes were lit with a mischievous light.

"Wanna stay?" he asked, searing her with his hungry look.

"Uh, no. I've got cooking to do."

"We could cook up something very special right here," he suggested, placing both hands on her shoulders and pulling her toward him. He rubbed his lips along her cheek, nibbling his way to the base of her throat.

"How special?" she murmured, happy to linger in his arms, enjoying the flare of desire that was spreading through her body.

"What about this?" he replied, kissing her hard on the lips, plunging his tongue deep into her mouth. "And this," he added slipping both hands beneath her blouse and into her bra to fondle her nugget-size nipples.

Lori's earlier arousal flared even hotter, sending her back into the dream scene that had vanished when she awoke. However, this was no dream. Ramón was in her house, his fingers were twirling her nipples and working her into a sweat that would only be cooled in a shower. He was also working his way into her heart, and she was surprised at how much she welcomed the intrusion. Stepping back, she sagged against the shower door and arched her shoulders back to give him better access to her breasts.

When he tore off her blouse and sent her bra to the bathroom floor, she groaned, knowing she was lost.

"Gotta get naked if you plan to join me," he taunted, shedding his clothes with two swift pulls that sent his jeans and his T-shirt to Lori's feet. Standing naked in front of her, she couldn't help but look down and gasp in appreciation at what she saw.

His family jewels were prominently displayed, standing at attention and ready to be admired. Unable to help herself, Lori reached down, ran her index finger along his shaft and then cupped his balls in the palm of her hand, handling him with care. Using her fingers as if she were playing the piano, she tapped her way back up to the tip and smiled when he groaned.

"You're killing me," he muttered, slipping down her slacks and helping her step out of them. With one arm holding on to her, he reached into the shower, turned on the water and pulled her into the stall, not caring that she was still wearing her thong underwear. As soon as the water hit Lori, he flattened her against the wall and smothered her with kisses, pressing his erection into her water-slick stomach.

Maintaining the kiss, Lori groped for the tube of shower gel she kept on the toiletry shower caddy, squirted a handful of the fragrant gel into her palm and then reached down to massage Ramón with both hands. Using a fistlike grip, she placed her thumbs at the base of his manhood and then slid her grip up and down his erection in slow, easy moves that quickly brought him to the brink of eruption.

"Ohmigod," Ramón groaned. "You gotta go all the way. Don't you dare stop."

And Lori didn't. She pressed his penis against her aching bud and continued to manipulate his throbbing tool. She rubbed the bubbly lather over him as he shouted in laughter, surprise and appreciation. Back and forth. Up and down. His flesh felt like warm satin between her palms. Lori worked him with sure, steady strokes until he exploded in her hand, gasped in relief and fell against the shower wall, limp with elation.

Lori kissed Ramón softly on the cheek and eased from beneath him. Stepping out of the shower, she began to towel off. Looking back at Ramón, she grinned and pointed to a stack of towels.

"Gotta go. Right now, any more cooking that's gonna happen will be in the kitchen, okay?" Laughing, she arched a brow at Ramón and then left him alone to take his shower, feeling smugly delighted that she'd pleasured him to satisfaction, that she'd had him under her control, if only for a few minutes. He might be the expert when it came to security devices, but she knew a thing or two about how to please a man.

Fifteen minutes later, Lori heard Ramón's footsteps behind her as he crossed the kitchen toward her, but she didn't turn around. Instead, she continued slicing cucumbers for her Italian salad, curious to see what he might do. When he suddenly rested his chin on her shoulder, the touch of his still-damp hair on her cheek initiated a surge of heat that made her heart turn over in response. Tilting back her head, she sliced off a thin round of the cool, pale vegetable. "Taste?" she offered, moving her hand toward his mouth.

Ramón took the cucumber slice between his teeth and then swept his tongue over her fingers, sucking on her fingertips and pulling them into his mouth as he took the vegetable in.

Lori turned, her fingers still between his lips, her body pressed to his. Smiling, she eased her hand away and watched him as he finished off the cucumber slice, her entire body flooded with an incredible sense of wanting. She'd satisfied him in the shower, but she'd walked out with her whole body on fire. Now the intensity of his gaze revved her impulse to make love to him, to satisfy the overpowering arousal she'd felt since awakening that morning.

"Very good," Ramón commented. "Fresh and delicious." He looked at her as if branding her with an intent to possess. "Kinda like you."

Lori scanned him with an exaggerated expression, mocking her offense. "Oh? You're comparing *me* to a cucumber?"

He touched her lips with his thumb and raked her with a bold dare of a stare. "Sure, your kisses taste so damn good and you're always so cool and calm."

A short laugh erupted as Lori lowered her line of vision. "Well, I can think of something else that would make a better comparison," she taunted, eyes trained on a certain part of Ramón's anatomy while waving the cucumber back and forth to emphasize her point.

"Aha, you may be on to something," he agreed, his voice gravelly and raw. "I'd love nothing more than to prove your theory."

"I might just let you," Lori replied, quite ready to satisfy her own needs, and a bit shocked by her own eagerness. She searched his face for assurance that he understood what she was telling him. His virile appeal was overwhelming, and she had no doubt that he was ready to meet her demands and perform as she hoped. However, her mind raced with concern. Was she soaring off into dangerous territory, climbing too high, too fast? Would she be better off stalling this incredible takeoff and keeping her feet on the ground a while longer?

"Well, what about a sneak preview of what to expect?" he insisted, his hands moving magically over her breasts.

"I...I guess an advance peek wouldn't hurt," she relented, yielding to his charm.

Ramón claimed her lips in a smooth, swift pass and pressed her firmly against the kitchen counter, demanding her attention in a strong, yet tender approach. His hand closed over the strap of her camisole, and Lori didn't resist when he slipped it off her shoulder. With her head braced against the kitchen cabinet and her hips lodged against her granite countertop, she snuggled into his embrace.

Ramón groaned, bent his head to kiss Lori's cheek and then hid his face against her neck while pressing his bulging member against her.

As if it had a mind of its own, Lori's hand eased down to capture the zipper of Ramón's jeans and quickly work it down. After releasing his stiff rod from its captivity, she caressed it with a series of slow lazy strokes, running her hand along its warm, throbbing shaft while luxuriating in the shudders of longing that rocked her body and ripped through her.

Ramón reached down, grabbed a condom from his pants pocket, and put it on. He cupped both of his hands under Lori's hips and lifted her up, forcing her to wrap her legs around his waist to keep from falling. With one hand around Ramón's neck and the other still caressing his enlarged sexual tool, Lori let herself be carried into her bedroom where he eased her down and hovered above her until she arched up to meet his lips.

Sinking into the soft coverlet, she relaxed while Ramón worked her hips out of her slacks and slipped her panties down. After pulling her camisole over her head, Ramón got naked just as fast. Giving in to the searing pulse of need that had been throbbing inside her all day, Lori opened herself completely to Ramón, moaning slightly when he entered, clamping her legs around his waist in a determined grip as she rode him hard until they both collapsed, panting, satisfied, quivering and gasping, in a tangle of sweat-drenched limbs.

# *Chapter 9*

"Is Detective Washington coming to the homeowners' meeting tonight?" Lori called over to Brittany after retrieving her morning paper from the lawn. She headed up the driveway while unfolding the Houston Chronicle. A week had passed since Brittany and her detective buddy had launched their community-watch program, and Lori wanted an update.

"Yep. And call him Clint. I do."

"So, it's progressed to first names, huh?" Lori teased.

"Honey, we passed first names a few nights ago."

Lori screwed her lips to the side and mocked her shock. "Fast workers, you two."

"Hey, you should talk," Brittany countered in a suggestive tone, a wicked smile spreading over her face. "Girlfriend, I know the security man has been at your house awfully late every night this week and I doubt you two are talking access codes and burglar bars." A beat. "Am I right or am I wrong?"

Lori's head snapped up and her heart started vibrating in her chest. It would be nice to spill all to Brittany and get her friend's perspective on whatever was happening, but Lori held back, not ready to turn her budding relationship with Ramón into girl-talk fodder for them to dissect. "I'll never tell," she skillfully teased, deciding to keep the full extent of her relationship with Ramón to herself a while longer.

How could she explain how an invitation to dinner had wound up with her pleasuring him in the shower? That they'd gone from sampling cucumbers in her kitchen to making sinfully sweet love in her bedroom? How could she describe the electrifying impact he was having on her or why, in the span of six days, she'd surrendered herself so completely to this man? His every touch sent her reeling with longing, forcing her to respond, sending her on passion-filled journeys to the most incredible heights she had ever experienced. Ramón had taken up residence in her heart, and Lori prayed she hadn't made a huge mistake by letting down her guard.

"You don't have to say anything," Brittany tossed back. "I can tell by the look on your face and the pep in your step that something special is going on."

"Maaaaybe," Lori hedged, a wistful expression tilting her lips up at the corners.

"Hey, go for it, Lori. Ramón is too damn cute to pass up, and handy in lots of ways, I presume?"

Lori swatted Brittany with her newspaper, chuckling as she turned back toward the house. "Brit, you need to quit."

"Okay, okay. Keep it to yourself, girlfriend. I've gotta get back to some phone calls I need to make. Want to walk over to the clubhouse with me later on?"

"Sure. What time?"

"Starts at seven," Brittany said as she crossed the driveway that separated her property from Lori's. "What about your security guy? He gonna drop in and promote his high-tech systems?"

"Ramón said he'd try to make it," Lori offered, glancing at the headlines on the newspaper to keep from looking at Brittany, who probably knew Ramón's truck never pulled out of Lori's driveway until close to dawn whenever he came over. "It's a pretty busy time for him right now, but he wants to fit us in."

"I'll bet he's been doing a good job of fitting something else in, too," Brittany blurted out over her laughter.

"Let's not go there, all right, Brit?" Lori cautioned. "I just hope we get a decent turnout and this homeowners' meeting doesn't wind up being a waste of time."

"Hey, I don't care who comes, as long as my Honey Bear Washington shows," Brittany stated with a zinger snap of her fingers.

The Brightwood Estates homeowners' meeting went smoothly, with the residents voting unanimously for Brittany Adams to be the captain of their community watch patrol, and for her to work closely with Detective Washington to implement their plan.

Ramón's presentation generated lots of interest in his security products, prompting several requests for him to review old alarm systems for possible updates.

After the meeting broke up, Ramón drove Lori home. When he pulled up to Lori's house, he shut the engine, leaned over and kissed her in a demanding press. "I've wanted to do that all evening. You have no idea how hard it was to keep focused on my presentation with you sitting in the front row, staring at me and looking so damn delicious."

"Hmm," she murmured, kissing him back. "I didn't mean to distract you. Just wanted to let you know I was paying attention."

"I got the message," he whispered, as she slithered out of his arms and popped open the door.

"Thanks for the ride home," she said, lingering on the sidewalk, still holding the truck's door open.

"No invite in?" he asked with a frown.

"Sorry, not tonight."

Ramón made a grunt to convey his disappointment, but sat back behind the wheel without complaint. "See you tomorrow, then?" he queried, expecting her to say yes.

"Can't," Lori tossed out rather nonchalantly. "I'm back to work tomorrow. Early call...off to Acapulco again. But we'll get together when I get back."

"I'm going to hold you to that," Ramón replied, blowing her a kiss as she shut the door and headed up the walkway.

Waiting in the driveway, he watched until Lori shut her front door, still surprised by how quickly he had become enamored of her. She was fun to be with, a free spirit who enjoyed an unencumbered lifestyle and seemed thrilled by what was developing between them. Ramón was not worried about Lori's no-strings-attached attitude. In fact, she was exactly what he needed: a beautiful, smart woman who could sex the hell out of him in bed with no desire to lock him down in a serious, all-consuming relationship. What else could he ask for? he wondered, zooming off down the street.

As soon as Ramón walked into his condo, his cell phone rang. Answering as he entered his den, he greeted Xavier, who began talking very fast in an uptight, nervous prattle.

"Slow down, bro," Ramón advised, perching on the corner of his brown leather sofa and zapping the remote to turn on his big-screen TV. Leaving the sound muted, he channel-surfed to the basketball game on ESPN while listening to what Xavier had to say.

"So what are you talking about?" Ramón inquired, certain he'd heard Xavier wrong.

"All I know is that his name is Aldo Lopez, and I'm telling you the truth, Ramón. He offered me $20,000 to validate and court-certify passports, IDs, social security cards and birth certificates. All to aid in smuggling people into the U.S."

"Hmm. You know what those the papers will be used for, don't you?"

"Of course. Fake ID's to get passports for some coyote who's running illegals across the border."

"Xavier, you need to inform the authorities."

"No way," Xavier refused. "Are you kidding? With as many dirty cops as there are in the force down here? That would be a death sentence."

"But you have to," Ramón insisted. "You can't jeopardize your job, your reputation. You'd lose everything you worked so hard to build if you went along with Lopez!"

"I know…I've already received a threatening phone call from him. I got his drift…my wife and daughter will suffer the consequences if I don't cooperate."

"So what are you gonna do?" Ramón asked, not liking what he was hearing.

"I'm not sure. But I do know I want you to come down and really tighten up the security on my property. I want the works. I've gotta keep Lopez from getting close to me or my family until I figure this thing out."

"I'll be on the first flight out tomorrow," Ramón promised, worried that a beefed-up security system might not be enough to protect his brother from a human trafficker out to do him harm.

# Chapter 10

When Lori emerged from the forward cabin, she was caught off guard to see Ramón sitting in the first-class cabin, beaming a devilish grin at her. His cool blue shirt, open at the neck, complimented his deep tan skin and provided a peek at the fine dark hair covering his chest. When his brown eyes raked her with a lingering scan, a tremor of expectation rippled through Lori, heightening her longing to feel him all over her again. She flashed a quick, professional smile at Ramón, tightened her grip on the Bloody Marys she handed to the couple in the first row and then took a moment to gather her composure.

Was it only a few days ago that she had lain naked in Ramón's arms, exhausted and fulfilled as their damp flesh cooled under the ceiling fan in her master bedroom? How could she have fallen so hard, so quickly? she wondered, moving down the center aisle toward him.

"What are you doing here?" she finally hissed, assessing him with a suspicious squint of both eyes.

Ramón tilted forward, one arm on his tray table as he whispered to her in a voice that should have been a lot softer.

"I'd like to say I'm here because I'm worried about your safety and I can't let you out of my sight, but..."

"Stop right there," Lori cautioned with a shushing sound. "I don't need constant watching. I don't want to be crowded. If this is what you think I like, then you're sadly mistaken." She sighed and glanced around, certain that everyone in the cabin had heard her, even though they were pretending to mind their own business.

"Hold on. You didn't let me finish," Ramón rushed to say. "I've got a security job to do in Acapulco, that's why I'm on your plane."

Straightening her spine, Lori jutted out her chin. "Oh? Really? Why didn't you tell me about it last night?"

"Because it didn't come up until after I dropped you off. I had to book a seat to Acapulco, so I decided to travel on your plane. On the flight we met, I overheard you saying to the other flight attendant that this was one of your regular flights. I wouldn't want anyone else taking care of *me,* would I?"

"Please," she responded with a flip of her hand, while giggling to let him know she wasn't really mad. "But you'd better behave yourself. I've got work to do." Turning away, Lori got busy helping an older woman who was trying to push her bag into the overhead bin.

"I see your Latin lover is back," Phyllis cattily commented as she squeezed past Lori with a blanket in her hand.

"Hmm, I know," Lori managed, tugging down her skirt after the lady's bag was safely stowed.

"And he's watching you like a cat pursuing a mouse," Phyllis observed, talking out of the side of her mouth as she handed the blanket to a passenger. "I guess you'll be going dancing tonight?"

"I doubt that. He's supposed to be working, and I certainly haven't made any plans to go out," Lori commented, while thinking that a repeat dance session with Ramón at Club Azule might be a lot of fun. Why not return to the place where this whirlwind relationship had started and slip into his arms, place her head on his shoulder, and let her thighs rub against his?

"But actually," Lori told Phyllis, "I had no idea he'd be on this flight."

"Well, he is, and it looks like he's waiting for you to pay him some attention," Phyllis finished, turning away from Lori to accept the passenger list from the boarding agent.

Though thrilled to have Ramón on board, Lori hoped he was telling her the truth about this trip. The last thing she wanted was to get involved with another possessive, clingy man, determined to control her every move. She'd been there, done that, with Devan Parker, and her nerves would never hold up through another experience like that.

Early in their relationship, she had been pleased when Devan flew on her flights—just to be near her, he'd said. Her route at the time had been Houston to LA, and Devan had traveled often to his company's offices in Los Angeles. The arrangement meant spending lots of free time together on the coast. At first, the meshing of their schedules had seemed perfectly normal: a lucky set of circumstances created by the demands of their jobs. However, when Lori discovered that Devan's marketing and public relations company did not have a West Coast office and that he had been flying on her shift so he could be close to her, she became uneasy.

She confronted him with the truth. He tried to dismiss his actions as a joke, insisting that he loved her so much she ought to understand. When he suggested that Lori stop flying and transfer to airport duties so she could stay in Houston to be near him, she knew something was not right.

Her suspicions were confirmed when Devan sprang an engagement ring on her after only six months of dating. He proudly informed Lori that once they got married, she would quit her job to take care of the home he planned to buy for her and the kids he planned to have.

Lori turned Devan down flat and offered him very little comfort when he called the next day to beg her, through tearful sobs, to reconsider his proposal. When she held fast, he became distraught and threatened to kill himself. Lori did not waver.

He started showing up at her house late at night, sitting in his car while talking to her on the phone. His aggressive campaign to get her to marry him included a deluge of e-mails, unannounced visits at her house and at the airport, late-night phone calls and so many flower deliveries she began to refuse them.

As each day passed and the situation deteriorated, Lori grew more nervous. When Brittany urged Lori to file a stalking charge against him and take out a temporary restraining order, she did. It worked. The judged ordered Devan into therapy to control his possessive urges and granted Lori's restraining order, ending a difficult time in her life.

With a mental shake, Lori cleared away disturbing memories of Devan Parker, eager to concentrate on the present. Ramón was the complete opposite of Devan. With Ramón, she could keep things light, noncommittal and exciting. Lori's work kept her on the go, but Ramón thought their frequent separations only made for more intense reunions. He would never try to clip her wings or make her conform to his demands. He understood her too well to try something like that.

Watching Lori walk up and down the center aisle as she performed her flight attendant duties was driving Ramón crazy. All he could think about was having her naked in his bed, sliding his hands over that soft, brown butt, inhaling her sexy, sultry scent. The sway of her hips, the tilt of her head, the way she spoke so sweetly to strangers in her charming voice sparked a stir of emotion that swelled inside Ramón and kept his attention riveted on Lori.

Having her so close, yet so untouchable, was pushing all the buttons he was trying to control. He was tempted to reach out and caress her thigh when she swept past him, or tickle the back of her leg when she paused to talk to the passenger across the aisle, touching that spot behind her knee that he knew would make her laugh. However, he couldn't do any of those things. All he could do was suffer in silence while his heart thumped in his chest and his stomach tightened in need.

Unable to stand it any longer, he ordered another drink. When Lori handed it to him, he made physical contact at last, tensing his fingers over her wrist and pulling her down when she leaned in to serve him. No longer concerned about what anyone on Globus-Americas flight 578 saw or thought, he planted a quick, hard kiss on her lips and then let her go.

Shocked, Lori straightened up and hurried into the forward galley, her back as stiff as a poker as she dodged out of sight.

Ramón chuckled, looked around and saw that the man across the aisle had seen what he did. Ramón shrugged. The man winked and gave Ramón a firm thumbs-up. Ramón sat back in his seat and grinned, knowing Lori Myles meant everything to him and that she was going to marry him. She just didn't know it yet.

## Chapter 11

Before touching down in Acapulco, Lori approached Ramón and stood in front of his seat, looking down at him.

"Wait for me in the terminal," she mouthed, not about trust a whisper.

"With pleasure," Ramón murmured, anticipating their reunion.

After deplaning, he waited at the gate until the flight crew had finished their final pass through the cabin and Lori emerged from the jetway, pulling her rolling bag behind her.

Ramón kissed her hello, slowly and gently, allowing his pent-up desire to escape. He ignored the curious glances of her crew, not caring who saw them together or what they thought. He was just happy to be in Mexico with Lori, even though he had come to work at his brother's house and she was on the clock, too. "Welcome to Acapulco," he joked.

"It's not like this is my first time here, you know?"

"I know, but it is the first time we've *arrived* together."

"True. And not by accident, either. I still can't believe you booked your flight on my plane without letting me know." She punched him lightly on the arm. "How much time do you think we'll be able to spend together? You came here to work, didn't you?"

"Let me worry about that," Ramón replied, taking her bag from her.

"Fine, but there's something else going on," Lori said, looking somewhat perplexed.

"What?" he asked. "Is something wrong?"

"The pilot just informed the crew that our plane has to undergo a mechanical check that's going to take at least an extra day."

"So what does that mean for you and the crew?" Ramón wanted to know.

"We don't leave tomorrow. I'm free until they call us back to work."

"Not bad," Ramón commented, smiling and guiding Lori away from the gate and into the terminal. "See? You and I are gonna have more time together than you thought."

"How? Aren't you working?" Lori said, falling in step with Ramón as they wove past the throng of people hurrying through the airport. "Ramón…" She paused to study him for a second. "You are telling me the truth about having a job to do in Acapulco, aren't you?" she pressed.

Ramón shot Lori a puzzled look, and then eased his arm around her waist to give her a quick hug. "Of course. Why would I make up something like that?"

"I don't know. Forget it," Lori dismissed with a shake of her head. "Just trying to keep you honest."

"Okaaaay. Well, here's the deal. My brother—the one who's now a judge—asked me to oversee the installation of a high-tech security system at his house. He lives on a huge estate on the bay, so he needs a pretty extensive setup."

"So you're staying with your brother at his estate while you're here?"

"Yeah. And I'm renting a car," Ramón replied.

"Great. Can you drop me at the Prince Hotel on Castaneda Street?" Lori asked, dodging a runaway toddler fleeing from his mother, who was juggling an infant and two carry-on bags. "Would that be out of your way?"

"No, but...why don't you come with me?"

"To your brother's house? Don't you think that would be an imposition?"

"Not at all. Xavier's cool. He and his wife, Carmen, love to have company. His house is as big as a luxury hotel and they thrive on having company. It could be fun," Ramón insisted as they approached the rental car counter.

"I dunno."

"Trust me. It'll be fine. I'll call and alert him, if you want."

"If you're sure it's okay," Lori hedged, uncertain about getting too close to Ramón's family. She certainly didn't want to give anyone the impression that their relationship was more serious than it was.

"Yeah, it's okay. Xavier's always telling me to bring my friends out to the house. Never had anyone I wanted to take—until now." Ramón pulled out his sunglasses and slid them over his eyes before turning to look back at Lori. "Xavier and I are very close. I want you to meet him and Carmen. They have a little girl—my only niece, Linda. She's a great kid. They're all the family I have in Mexico, and I enjoy spending time with them."

"Well, okay, I'll go, but I have to let Phyllis, our flight leader, know where I can be reached."

"Good, that's settled. You call Phyllis while I call Xavier and get the car," he decided, taking the car-rental papers from the attendant. "Tell her you'll be at Villa Marquesa on Tropicana Road. The phone number is—" He paused to take out his cell phone to scroll through the address book.

"That's okay—" Lori stopped Ramón with a touch to his hand "—I don't need the number. Phyllis can reach me on my cell," Lori told him, looking forward to meeting Ramón's brother and his family.

While she had been getting dressed for work that morning, she had dreaded the upcoming time away from Ramón, anticipating an uneventful trip out and back, never dreaming she'd wind up having an unexpected romantic escape with him in Acapulco.

Xavier Vidal's villa by the sea was a majestic white stucco Mediterranean-style house, nestled in the lush vegetation and rolling hills bordering Acapulco Bay. Its spectacular ocean view and natural waterfalls made Lori think she had arrived at the entrance to a lush botanical garden. Blindingly white and pristine, the arched windows in the three-story home were draped with cascades of hot pink blooms that created a vibrant shower of color.

As soon as Ramón parked the car in the circular driveway, Xavier's front door flew open and a man who bore a striking resemblance to Ramón rushed down the white stone steps to welcome them. Lori was immediately taken by Xavier's boisterous charm as he pumped her hand in greeting. Though it was clear that Xavier was the elder of the two brothers, his youthful physique and energetic manner made Lori think they could have passed as twins.

"Come in, come in!" Xavier called out, guiding Lori and Ramón up the stairs, into the house, down a hallway lined with art-filled niches and into a sun-splashed room with a spectacular view of the ocean.

"Hello!" a voice came out from across the room as soon as they entered.

"This is my wife, Carmen," Xavier said, extending his arm toward a model-gorgeous woman whose statuesque beauty was breathtaking. Raven-haired, slim, willowy and soft-spoken, Carmen hugged Ramón and then hugged Lori, welcoming her with genuine delight in heavily accented English. With introductions made, they chatted about the view until a little girl appeared in her swimsuit and greeted Ramón excitedly.

"This is Linda, our daughter," Carmen told Lori. "And as you can see she's eager to get to the pool."

Lori looked beyond the wall of glass that surrounded the back part of the house and focused on the tropically landscaped aqua-blue pool. "I can understand why," Lori commented, smiling at Linda, shifting closer to the windows. "What a beautiful place to swim!"

"You guys wanna come?" Linda asked, eyeing Ramón as if daring him to say no. She hugged her beach towel across her shoulders and waited for an answer.

"I think Ramón and his friend might want to rest for a while.

They just arrived from Houston," Carmen intercepted, smiling at the dark-haired girl who was the spitting image of her mother.

"But maybe later," Lori offered in consolation.

"Okay. Nice to meet you," Linda called out before scurrying out of the room.

"She's so cute," Lori remarked.

"Spoiled rotten. A true Daddy's little girl," Carmen replied with a hint of pride. "Now. I understand you're a flight attendant… with an unexpected layover?"

"Right," Lori agreed. "Houston to Acapulco is my regular run. I rarely have time to get this far outside the city, so this is a real treat for me."

"I'm so happy Ramón brought you out for a visit. We're kind of isolated here, so it'll be good to have some company for a few days," Carmen said.

Xavier nodded his agreement, and then tapped Ramón on the arm. "Lori, you make yourself at home while Ramón and I take care of some business." He lowered his head and looked up at Ramón through skeptical eyes. "That *is* why you're here, remember?"

"Absolutely. Let's get busy installing that new alarm system you want," Ramón said as he and Xavier left the room.

"Would you like to see the rest of the house?" Carmen asked Lori.

"I'd love to," Lori replied, following Carmen on a brief tour of the estate. "What's this area called?"

"We're in Brisas Marqués, one the city's prettiest suburban areas. We've been here two years, but I still feel as if I just moved in. We love the privacy and the quiet away from the city."

Lori had never seen such a beautiful place. Located on a cliff overlooking the ocean, the villa consisted of three levels built around a series of waterfalls that carried water from the foyer of the house, through the living area, and on to the oceanside pool, where Linda was happily splashing around. Decorated in maximum luxury, the house had wide-screen TVs in every room, stereo music piped throughout, a home-theater system and billiards in the game room, a huge black marble bar and a fitness room with a private steam bath. Each of the five bedroom suites had bathrooms with large Jacuzzi-style bathtubs and multijet showers.

"We're always glad to see Ramón, and any of his friends are welcome. However, I have to say you are the first woman he has brought to meet us," Carmen told Lori as they stepped outside onto the lower patio overlooking Acapulco Bay. "Have you known Ramón a long time?"

"Two weeks, to be exact."

"Oh. I thought you've been friends a long time. You seem so at ease together."

"He's easy to be around, and I think I'm getting used to him."

"He's such a thoughtful, sincere young man. You're lucky. He seems to care a lot for you."

"Lucky? Yes, I guess so. It just feels like everything is moving so fast."

"Don't fret about anything. Enjoy the moment. That's the only way to live."

"You know, that's how I feel, too. Maybe that's why I feel so safe with Ramón, even though we haven't known each other very long."

"He's the best. I love him as much as if he were my blood brother, you know?"

Lori simply nodded.

"And I can guarantee that Ramón will always treat you right. He's a gentleman through and through."

"I totally agree," Lori admitted, letting her worries about showing up unannounced slip away. Carmen seemed genuinely happy to have an unexpected guest and this impromptu visit might be just what Lori needed to learn more about the man who was gaining fast on her heart.

## Chapter 12

"This looks very good," Ramón remarked as he inspected the new security fence that Xavier had installed. "It's top of the line, very reliable. And with a manned guardhouse at the entry, you ought to be fine. But what about access from the beach?" Ramón scanned the lush green lawn that sloped down toward the blue-green ocean.

"I have two guards with dogs patrolling the beach around the clock."

"Good. So where do things stand with Lopez and his demands?" Ramón wanted to know.

Xavier let out a groan and shook his head, looking worried. "I did as you suggested and went to the authorities. Had a long talk with Calderón, the Guerrero chief of police."

"Good place to start," Ramón replied with a tinge of relief. "Getting the authorities involved takes the heat off you, Xavier. Let the police track the guy down and find out what's going on. You have a court to run, professional responsibilities to fulfill, a family to think of. You don't need any more pressure."

A curt laugh flew from Xavier's lips. "Ha! Pressure? Listen

to this. Calderón wants me to wear a wire, meet with Lopez and take the money. I'm supposed to act like I'm going along with the deal so the police can infiltrate this fake ID ring."

"What?" Ramón stopped in his tracks and peered at Xavier, clearly upset to hear this news. "Do you know how dangerous that could be?"

With a nod, Xavier moved into a shady spot beneath a huge banana tree and leaned against its trunk. "Yeah, I do. But what choice to I have? The plan is for me to meet with Lopez next week, accept the fake documents, certify them and take the money. I'm supposed to keep tapes of the transactions in my safe so they can be used as evidence later on."

"At a criminal trial, I suppose?" Ramón inquired.

"That's the plan."

"Why not hand them over to the police right away? Why keep them in your home?"

"Because Calderón is certain that Lopez has people inside the police department. He doesn't want to take a chance on blowing my cover. I have to keep the tapes here under constant protection until he gives me the word to hand them over. That's why I need your help."

"I can upgrade the entry alarm to your house into one that is virtually impenetrable, but it will be complicated, expensive and difficult to install."

"But you can do it?"

"Sure. Might take a few days and I'll have to tear out a wall or two to get it all in place."

"I don't care about that, or the cost."

"Does Carmen know anything about what's going on?" Ramón asked.

"No. Nothing. And please don't mention anything to her, or anyone else. I don't want her to panic. When everything is locked down and the police are ready to make their move, I'll tell her. Until then, this has to stay between you and me."

Ramón shook his head in agreement. "I'm in the security business. I know how to keep my mouth shut. "Ramón stepped closer to Xavier and paused for a moment. "To make sure no one gets in your house who does not belong there and that your personal safe is absolutely tamperproof, we'll have to go biometric," he added.

"Biometric? What's that?" Xavier wanted to know.

"It means using a series of security devices to authenticate a person's identity on the basis of physical characteristics."

"Like a fingerprint?"

"Right. Or an eye scan or a voice print."

"You can do that?"

"Absolutely," Ramón confirmed.

"Okay, then that's the way we'll go," Xavier said, motioning for Ramón to follow him back toward the house. "Let's do this in my study. I'll show you where the safe is."

"Fine," Ramón said, walking alongside his brother. "I have to admit that even though I don't like what you're doing, I'm proud of you for cooperating with the police."

"Let's hope things don't get too nasty," Xavier threw back. "You know, I sympathize with people who want to emigrate to America, but they have to do it legally."

"I hear you. As our parents did when they moved to Texas," Ramón commented.

"Exactly."

"All Pop talked about during our last visit was how glad he is that we were able to grow up and be educated in Texas, but still maintain our connection to Mexico."

"I know. The courts on both sides of the border are packed with people caught up in the system because they tried to cross illegally. I sympathize with them, but I've got to do whatever I can to keep people like Lopez from exploiting them."

"It's all you can do," Ramón agreed. "Just be careful, okay? Lopez sounds like a pretty dangerous character."

The hot Acapulco sun was blazing down on the bay when Xavier and Ramón emerged from the house to rejoin the women on the patio.

"Now, isn't this much better than a hotel room in town?" Ramón remarked, walking over to Lori, who was seated across from Carmen under a patio umbrella. He perched on the arm of Lori's white wrought-iron chair and slid his hand across her shoulders in a possessive move that let everyone know how he felt about her.

"Of course it is. This place is gorgeous," Lori replied, suddenly struck by a strong sense that she had done the right thing by accompanying Ramón to Xavier's. She didn't feel the least bit awkward or out of place. In fact, she felt right at home.

"That's why I wanted you to come with me," Ramón said, giving her shoulder a squeeze.

Carmen smirked at him with a teasing grin. "Tell the truth, Ramón. Is that the only reason?" she wagged a finger at him. "This is a very beautiful young woman you have brought to meet us."

"Well, maybe not the only reason," he sheepishly admitted, glancing from Lori to Xavier and then back to Carmen. "Guess I didn't want to let her out of my sight."

"And I can understand why," Xavier boomed out as he threw an admiring look at Lori.

A short lull followed his remark, before Carmen announced, "As you saw, Lori, we have more than a few empty bedrooms around here, so you and Ramón will not be in our way at all. In fact, you'll probably have more privacy here than you'd have in a busy hotel in town."

Lori coughed under her breath, making an unintelligible sound in the back of her throat, aware of Carmen's inference that they must be sexually involved and would want some private space. Luckily, a response to Carmen's comment was deferred when a slightly rotund woman dressed in a black and white maid's uniform appeared at the patio entryway to announce that lunch was ready.

With a crook of her finger, Carmen summoned the woman closer. "Darla, Ramón and his friend, Ms. Myles, will use the master suite on the east wing. Make sure everything is as it should be and their bags are taken there, all right?"

"Yes, Mrs. Vidal. Right away," the maid replied, nodding at Ramón and then at Lori before leaving the patio to ready the rooms.

Lori cast a furtive glance at Ramón, who shrugged one

shoulder and gave her a cautious smile. Turning to Carmen, she said, "I don't want you to think—" then she floundered, unsure of how to tell Carmen that she and Ramón were not joined at the hip and that separate rooms would be just fine with her "—I don't want you to think that…I mean, Ramón and I are not…" she paused, throwing a fierce signal for help at Ramón.

"We're not living together or anything like that," he clarified for his sister-in-law.

"Right," Lori echoed in defense.

"At least, not yet," Ramón added with an amused expression.

"Ramón!" Lori called out, shaking her head in dismay. "What a thing to say!"

"Hey, I understand completely," Carmen said, clearly not concerned about the intensity of Ramón and Lori's relationship. "The suite has two bedrooms and a connecting bath. How you two use the space is not my concern. No need to say another word." With a chuckle, she led everyone inside to a white linen-draped table and motioned for them to sit down for lunch.

"This looks delicious," Lori said, taking in the spread of fruit, seafood pasta and vibrantly colored vegetables. She chose a seat, let Ramón help her settle in and then shook out her large white napkin.

"I know we're going to be good friends," Carmen said to Lori as she unfurled her napkin. "Now tell me how you two met."

Between bites of the lobster and shrimp salad, Lori, with Ramón's help, told Xavier and Carmen how they had met in the club in Acapulco.

"It was a real shock to find Lori working as a flight attendant on my return flight home," Ramón finished.

"It was fated," Xavier calmly observed as he tore off a piece of hot garlic bread and popped it into his mouth.

"Yes, sounds like you two were meant to be," Carmen wisely commented, sipping her raspberry iced tea. "And since that's the case, I hope we'll see a lot more of you from now on, Lori."

Lori cut her eyes at Ramón, who was beaming his support. After taking a long breath, she grinned at Carmen. "You know, I hope so, too."

# Chapter 13

After a family dinner of grilled steak and new potatoes, Ramón and Xavier spent the remainder of the evening working out kinks in the biometrics security devices he was installing. But once the house was quiet and everyone was settled for the night, Ramón was determined to spend some quiet time with Lori. He walked out onto the veranda that linked his bedroom to hers, stretched his neck and watched Lori, who had opted for a late-night dip in the pool, emerge from the dark blue water. Now he wished he'd been able to join her for a swim. "Maybe tomorrow," he murmured, his mind lurching ahead as he grasped for a reason to keep her in Acapulco as long as possible.

Xavier, Carmen and even little Linda had taken to Lori as if she were already a member of the family. Despite their cultural differences, she had easily slipped into the rhythm of their lifestyle, a fact that pleased Ramón immensely. He should not have been surprised at her ability to fit in with his family so effortlessly: she was a flight attendant, after all, and it was her job to make strangers feel at home. She was a true woman of the world; an adventurer with the kind of intellectual curiosity that accepted people for who and what they were without any pretense or hidden agendas. This was the woman he'd been searching for, even though he hadn't known it.

Now just looking at Lori made Ramón smile. He watched her approach the house, his heart thundering under his loose white shirt. It wasn't just the way her shapely body filled out her red bikini or the regal tilt of her head as she strode toward him that made his heart turn over. It was her charisma, her easy approach to life and her energetic sense of adventure that made the sight of her stunning silhouette against the moonlight hold him riveted in place.

Lori walked right up to Ramón and stopped. Without hesitation, he gripped her at the waist and moved her body up to meet his. He ran his hands down the curve of her spine, rippling his fingers over her damp flesh, not caring that her swimsuit was wet and her hair was dripping water. All he wanted to do was drink in the cool touch of her skin and savor the exquisite sensation of being alone with her on this dark, private veranda under a huge Mexican moon. The scene was heaven-made, and he planned to take advantage of this rare and beautiful moment.

Lori glanced up at Ramón and her face dissolved into an enormously attractive smile. "Hey, be careful. I'm all wet," she warned.

"Don't worry about me. I won't melt," he threw back, giving her a firm squeeze.

"I hope not," she joked. "I wouldn't want you disappearin' on me."

"I won't. I promise." He placed a tender peck on her lips. "Enjoy your swim?" he asked, startled by the undertone of roughness in his voice.

"Very much," she replied, turning within Ramón's embrace to snuggle her head beneath his chin and face the moon-glazed water.

A thrill of adrenaline shot through Ramón as he held on to Lori and let her presence sink into him. "Glad you came with me?" he prompted, nuzzling her cheek, his fingers entwined in her soft damp hair.

"Oh, yes. This minivacation was so unexpected, but exactly

what I need. The house, the grounds, the waterfalls—this is all very serene. I've been so stressed out since the break-in, I didn't realize how tense I was. And now I feel like I'm in the middle of a dream." She reached up to caress Ramón's cheek with one hand, trailing her fingertips over his lips. "Thanks for bringing me along to meet your family, Ramón. Xavier and Carmen have been so gracious in spite of my unexpected imposition."

Ramón leaned in and placed his chin on Lori's shoulder, his mouth only inches from her ear. "You didn't impose," he whispered.

"Okay, but still. They hardly…"

"Shhh…no more talk about that. You're my guest, so you're my brother's guest, too. In Mexico, it's all the same. *Mi casa es tu casa,* right?"

"Right," Lori relented, breaking their embrace to shift around, face him once more and take his hand in hers. "Carmen's a dear and your brother is quite the success. I understand why you're so proud of him. Plus, I don't know when I've enjoyed myself so much." Her eyes lingered on his face, her expression emphasizing her contentment.

The transparency of her emotions pushed Ramón's feelings for Lori into high gear, increasing the pace of his already rapid pulse. A strong throb of need drummed through his veins, churning up visions of Lori lying naked on the cool white sheets of her king-size bed, of his body covering hers, of the sparks they'd create once they were joined. Unable to restrain himself a moment longer, he captured the straps of Lori's bikini top between two fingers and began to ease them off her shoulders.

"Tell me what you're thinking," he whispered, glad she did not resist his effort to maneuver her out of her bikini top.

Lori took a moment to consider his question. "I wasn't thinking about anything in particular. Just enjoying the night. The stars, the breeze, the heavenly scent of the flowers in the garden, and… and being here with you, of course."

"It is a beautiful night, but not nearly as beautiful as the sight of you…standing there in the moonlight." He kissed the soft spot at the base of Lori's throat and then looked up, his hands making their way around to the swell of her buttocks. He spread his fingers over her hips and urged her closer, crushing her bare nipples against his chest. "But I'll bet you've been to more exotic places than this, huh?"

Lori reacted to Ramón's remark with a quick lift of her chin. "Sure, I've traveled all over Europe and most of Asia. I've met great people and seen some wonderful sights. But I have to admit that this trip is the one I'll remember most."

"Why?" Ramón asked, casually working to push down her bikini bottom, appreciating Lori's side-to-side wiggles that speeded his effort to undress her.

"Because you're here, and when I'm with you, I don't care about anything but experiencing every bit of you, taking advantage of your incredible ability to rock my world," she answered, eyes roaming his face.

Ramón gave the triangle of wet fabric covering her hips a swift tug and let it fall to her feet. "Exactly what I wanted to hear," he murmured in a voice that was thick with longing as he swept Lori up and into his arms. She wrapped her legs around his hips and pressed her naked core into him as he carried her inside.

For a brief blissful moment, he could only stare at Lori as she lay naked in the middle of her bed, her deep bronze skin glowing under the sheen of moonlight streaming through the wall of glass facing the sea. He felt comforted by the silence that drifted easily between them. She was relaxed, responsive and ready to be loved—the perfect set of circumstances for a tender seaside encounter.

After slipping out of his shirt and slacks, Ramón eased down beside Lori and assessed her magnificent pose. Her full breasts demanded his attention—plump heavy orbs of scented flesh that beckoned him to taste. He captured an erect brown nipple in his lips and suckled it until Lori squirmed in delight and gasped in pleasure. Shifting to the other breast, he repeated his sensuous lick-and-tug maneuvers, loving the taste of her flesh. He inhaled deeply, drawing in her essence, eager to sample more of it.

Lori's eyes lingered with longing on Ramón's chiseled profile as she watched him lick and tease the tip of her nipple, fully engaged in his delicious foreplay. She smothered a cry of delight when the wetness of his kisses caused a deep tug of pleasure that contracted her vaginal walls. She stretched her spine, pressed her body deeper into the soft covering on the bed, ready to capitulate completely to Ramón's exquisite touch. The whispering echo of the dark black sea wafted into the airy room, lulling Lori into a dreamlike state that intensified her longing to surrender. Was this all for real? she wondered silently. In his arms, she felt totally alive, eager to explore the future and anxious to see where they were headed. It seemed as if she had known Ramón Vidal for years, not weeks. And how crazy was that? she thought, loving the exotic, foreign setting for her thrilling encounter with this handsome, gentle man. To be in Acapulco with someone who intrigued her, knew how to pleasure her and wanted to have a good time seemed perfectly natural and in keeping with her love of adventure and her need to be free.

With one leg bent at the knee and the other languidly stretched to one side, Lori was opening herself to Ramón completely. Running his hand over the undulating sweep of her tight stomach, he felt his already hard member grow even more rigid. Ramón worked his hand down into the triangle of dark curly hair between Lori's thighs and inserted his middle finger into her core. With a jerk, she arched upward, but did not pull back, letting him know he was on the right track. With her hips slightly raised, she presented him with perfect access to her throbbing bud, which he took between his lips and twirled with his tongue. Faster and faster he lip-massaged her honey-slick essence while his finger drove deeper and deeper into her core. With a slight shift, Lori scooted lower. Ramón slipped his slippery fingers out and allowed Lori's thighs to hold him in place as she thrust her buttocks forward with each delicious lick and tug of his tongue. Determined not to break his rhythm or make Lori miss the climax she deserved, he pulled back, opened his mouth wide, and flicked his tongue back and forth over her sweet bud until she cried out, grasped his head with both hands and pressed it hard into the V of her legs, shuddering as she exploded in spasms of release in surrender to Ramón's expert titillation.

When Ramón lifted his head and gazed at her with probing, questioning eyes, she reached down and caressed his cheek with a tender cup of her fingers. Giving him a slow, languid blink, she silently urged him to proceed with his exploring moves, knowing she was slick with longing, hot with need and primed for penetration. Peeking down, she admired his handsome penis, which was smooth, erect and framed in a border of dark soft hair, ready to please her. Tenderly, yet insistently, she traced her fingers in wondrous reverence over his warm shaft until he moved to mount her, easing her legs apart with one knee.

Wrapping her legs around his back, she positioned herself under his stiff rod and let him sink down on her, emitting a moan of delight as he settled in. She threw back her head and opened herself to deeper penetration. With Ramón's hand beneath her hips, he held her pelvis in place as they began their climb toward total fulfillment.

The journey started slowly, in a sensuous, gentle probe that progressed inch by inch as he drove deeper and she gave him every reason to advance. Rocking beneath him, Lori let Ramón fill her up and sweep her away, loving the way he pleasured her.

"Oh, my," she murmured several times, as his inventive thrusts aroused her to the point of screaming. "Give it to me," she urged, pressing closer, determined to ride every inch of his astoundingly hard penis.

As the Acapulco waves crashed against the shoreline and the moonlight bathed them in tropical splendor, they bucked and rocked and hovered at the edge of climax again and again, teasing their bodies to see how far they could go before hitting the button that would cause the ultimate explosion. As their hot panting broke into the stillness of the night, they nuzzled and kissed and joined together in rhythmic plunges of connection until they melted like liquid gold into a single, exquisite explosion.

# Chapter 14

Morning sunlight warmed Lori's face and woke her with a sweep of light that brightened the dim bedroom. She shifted onto her side and lazily extended an arm, expecting to find Ramón slumbering next to her, but all she felt was empty space. Opening one eye, she checked the pillow that still had the indentation of his head in it and stuck out her bottom lip. Damn! He was gone. But his scent, mingled with the fragrance of their all-night lovemaking session, drifted from the sheets and sent a shiver of pleasure to the spot between her legs—the spot that Ramón had so recently vacated. Squeezing her thighs together, Lori breathed in a slow stream of air and held it in her lungs for a long moment, wishing Ramón had stayed around to continue what they'd been doing last night, and to sex her to satisfaction once more.

Sitting up, Lori blinked away the last vestiges of sleep and looked around the beautifully decorated bedroom, getting her bearings as she settled against the headboard. Yes, she was still in Acapulco, still in Ramón's brother's beautiful home, still in paradise with a man who was rocking her world in ways that shocked her, pleased her, but also caused concern.

*Sex is one thing. Falling in love is another. And you'd better keep the two as far apart as possible,* Lori silently cautioned herself, knowing her fun-in-the-sun escape with Ramón had to remain just that: a wonderful affair to remember, with no future entanglements or complications. *You've gotta keep the drama out of this one,* she told herself, not about to repeat what she had gone through the last time she let a man get under her skin. Ending a relationship was even harder than starting one, and she had no plans of going there again.

Lori pushed those thoughts aside and scanned the room, grinning to see her discarded bikini bottom hanging on the bedpost. Lori chuckled aloud, knowing Ramón must have put it there as a reminder of what had happened the night before…or what was to still come.

She squirmed lower into the covers, thinking back to the erotic journey she and Ramón had taken together. *Incredible* was the only word to describe the way he'd used his hands, his fingers and his inventive tongue in tandem with his oh-so-perfect manhood to bring her such exquisite release. For the first time in her adult life, she'd had four orgasms in one night, with the force of each explosive climax leaving her weak, but hungry for another. Her clitoris still throbbed from the extensive workout it had received, and it was still sending tiny pulses of need through Lori, as if calling for another round of Ramón's sumptuous stimulation.

Lori, who had never taken drugs in her life, now wondered if this was how addicts felt when they needed a fix. While in Ramón's arms, she felt addicted—craving him, needing him and ready to go beyond her comfort zone to achieve that elusive sense of pitch-perfect pleasure. As he'd pushed their sexual encounter to ever higher and higher levels, Lori had been inspired to reciprocate by making moves on Ramón she'd never tried before. The taste of his natural maleness still lingered in her mouth, along with the sensation of his thighs clamped hard against her cheeks when she brought him over the edge. He'd stiffened, stifling his cry of pleasure while pressing her head so deep and hard into him that she'd temporarily lost her breath.

A knock on the door startled Lori from her thoughts and, looking over at the entryway, she reached for the soft pink robe on the bedside chair and slipped it over her shoulders. "Yes?" she called out, one eyebrow raised as she wrapped the soft fabric over her naked breasts and then tied the robe at her waist.

The maid, Darla, entered, carrying what looked like a very full breakfast tray.

"Oh, my. You didn't have to do that," Lori protested, half rising from her bed.

Darla grinned at Lori in a most mischievous manner. "Mr. Ramón went with Mr. Xavier this morning to pick up the electrician. He told me to be sure to bring you breakfast in bed so you can enjoy watching the boats gather on the bay. It's a colorful parade when the yachts and sailboats arrive, and this room has such a beautiful view." Darla placed the tray of food on a table just outside the patio door, and then turned around and faced Lori. "Oh, and he said to tell you he'd be back about ten."

"Fine," Lori commented lightly, though disappointed that Ramón would not be there to enjoy breakfast with her. However, she knew he'd come to Acapulco to work, not to fool around with her, even though they'd gotten in a pretty good session last night. Anyway, she wasn't on vacation, either. She'd be back on the plane soon serving passengers, leaving Ramón behind to complete the work he was doing on his brother's house.

Focusing on Darla, Lori nodded her appreciation. "This looks delicious. Thank you so much."

Sitting on the patio, Lori enjoyed a wonderful Mexican breakfast of huevos rancheros and chorizo. Finished eating, she phoned Phyllis to check on the status of their departure, not wanting her short, and unexpected, vacation to end.

"What's the plan?" she asked when Phyllis answered.

"We have another change," Phyllis replied, going on to tell Lori that their plane remained grounded, but the crew was cleared to depart Acapulco on another flight later in the day.

"Is this a mandatory return?" Lori wanted to know, hoping to squeeze in an extra day in Acapulco.

"Not mandatory, and since you're due twenty-four hours off, you can either return to Houston on the ferry flight with the rest of the crew or stay behind."

"Really?" Lori replied, her mind already processing her decision. She wanted to spend one more day with Ramón, so this was the answer to her prayers. "Think I'll stick around and work the return flight when repairs are complete. What are you going to do?" Lori wanted to know.

"I'm taking the ferry back today," Phyllis replied. "By the way, why are you at Villa Marquesa, exactly?"

"I'm at Ramón's brother's house."

"Okay. Now, I understand why you're not so eager to leave. Things must be moving pretty fast, huh?"

"No, not really. We're just having fun."

"Okaaaay. Using all this extra time to get to know each other better?"

Lori considered Phyllis's remark. "Yes. That's true. And I'm getting to know his family, too. His brother is very nice. The house is absolutely gorgeous. I feel like I'm at a luxury resort hotel," Lori divulged.

"I'm jealous," Phyllis joked. "You get to enjoy a getaway with a gorgeous Latin hunk, while I watch bullfights on Mexican TV in a two-star hotel."

"All right, Phyllis. Staying in…that's your choice," Lori threw back. "No one is holding you prisoner in the hotel. I keep telling you, you need to get out and explore. Meet new people. Don't be so afraid of having a little adventure. You're the most cautious flight attendant I ever met."

"Easy for you to say. Honey, I've survived in this business this long because I'm cautious by nature. Risky behavior has never tempted me, and at my age, I doubt I'd still be flying if I'd taken advantage of every opportunity to break loose in every city I visited."

"You do what suits you, and I do what makes me happy," Lori commented, not wanting to be lectured by Phyllis, who wore her low-risk lifestyle like a badge of honor while throwing a damper on everyone else's good time.

"So what are you doing tonight?" Phyllis probed. "Dancing the night away with Mr. Hunk?"

"Uh, no. And please…his name is Ramón Vidal."

"Okay, Ramón. Didn't you say he's a security expert or something?"

"Yes. He came to Acapulco to install a new system in his brother's house."

"The one who owns the villa," Phyllis clarified.

"Yeah, the federal judge."

"Oh, yeah. And what's his name again?"

"Xavier Vidal. And from what I understand, he's a pretty important guy around here."

"Hmm, I'm impressed," Phyllis said. "Sounds like you might be onto a good thing this time."

"I'm hanging loose, Phyllis. And Ramón is, too."

"All right. If you say so. Well, I've gotta go. See you back in Houston."

"Right," Lori said as she ended the call, feeling unsettled by her conversation with Phyllis, who'd seemed unusually interested in the progress of Lori's relationship with Ramón.

Even though Lori had worked with Phyllis over the past four years, she still had trouble reading her. Phyllis could switch from girlfriend-friendly to boss-woman-cool in a matter of seconds. Lori knew she had better draw the line with Phyllis and keep their relationship on a professional level. That took priority over personal chitchat about intimate matters.

Crossing her legs, Lori sat back in her patio chair and studied the sleek white yachts and sailboats sliding across the water, already planning her next adventure with Ramón.

"Great news," Carmen commented after learning that Lori did not have to leave right away. "We get to keep you here an extra day." Carmen slid her sunglasses over her eyes and picked up her Prada purse. "I'm on my way into town for my yoga class and spa treatment. I'll be gone until late this afternoon, but Xavier and Ramón are due back any moment. In fact, I think I hear them now."

Lori glanced out the large bay window that faced the circular drive and saw Xavier's black Mercedes come to a stop.

"Gotta go. Have fun. We'll have dinner by the pool tonight,"

Carmen told Lori, giving her a hug and leaving the room just as Ramón and Xavier entered.

After Lori explained the change in her plans, Xavier took charge of the situation. "I'll stay here while the electrician runs the new wiring, so Ramón can take you out and show you more of our lovely countryside."

"Sounds perfect," Lori commented, a hopeful expression on her face. "Can you do that?" she asked Ramón, not wanting to take him away from something he had to do.

"Of course. The first phase of my work here is done, and I can't do anything else until the electrician finishes. So sure. Let's go."

"Fantastic," Lori agreed, now turning to Xavier. "Any suggestions?"

"Absolutely," Xavier said. "I insist you take a cruise around the bay on *La Princesa*."

"*La Princesa?*" Lori repeated, glancing from Xavier to Ramón.

"My yacht," Xavier said with pride as he crossed his elegant living room and went to an antique desk next to the fireplace. He opened a small inside drawer and took out a key. "Ramón, you know where *La Princesa* is berthed. Here are the inside cabin keys. I'll give the marina a call so everything will be ready when you two get there." He clapped a hand on Ramón's shoulder in a display of brotherly confidence and affection. "Show this lovely lady a good time, you hear?"

"I will," Ramón promised, winking at Lori.

Arriving at Lago Acapulco Marina, Lori's mouth dropped open when she saw Xavier's luxury vessel gleaming sleek and white in its slip in the harbor, which was only a fifteen-minute drive from the judge's house. And once they boarded *La Princesa*, her jaw opened even wider as Ramón gave her a tour of the ultramodern vessel.

"Carmen's father is a big-time banker in Argentina. He gave *La Princesa* to her and Xavier as their wedding present," Ramón explained, leading Lori into the main salon.

"How beautiful," Lori murmured, reaching out to touch the paneled walls that gave a rich, cozy feel to the room.

"Honduran mahogany," Ramón informed. "Imported especially for this yacht."

"Really?" Lori murmured, admiring the walls, the butter-cream leather upholstery on the large wraparound settee, the marble-topped side tables and brass Stiffel lamps. Inlaid hardwood floors and custom silk window coverings matched the cushions on the chairs. A big-screen TV and state-of-the-art sound system completed the amenities in the grand salon. All the interior appointments created a sense of high drama, and though the opulent yacht was elegant, it was surprisingly compact and efficient-looking, with built-in cabinets that gleamed beneath recessed lights that cast a soft yellow glow over everything.

Ramón went to consult with the captain about their minicruise while Lori explored the rest of the yacht. When she entered the bathroom, she was not surprised to see that it was truly worthy of a princess. Blue and white veined marble floor, Jacuzzi tub with sauna, gold-toned fixtures, and eye-catching blue granite counters greeted her.

"Wow" was all she could say as she finished in the bathroom and ventured into the corridor leading to the master stateroom. Glancing around, she marveled at the intoxicating swirl of blue and turquoise in shimmering iridescent shades of green that had been used on the window coverings, upholstery and bed linens. Oil paintings that looked like they were done by authentic old masters adorned the walls and a chandelier with crystal teardrop prisms dangled above the king-size bed.

"Ramón and I could certainly cut loose in here," she murmured, a sly smile coming over her lips. The image of the two of them cocooned in the luxurious aqua satin sheets, wrapped in each other's arms, flashed into her mind with such intensity, her heart turned over in anticipation.

# Chapter 15

As the languorous day slipped past, Ramón and Lori cruised Acapulco Bay, ogling the mansion-size villas along the shore and waving to fellow yachters. They went ashore to shop in an open market where Lori bought a fuchsia straw hat for Brittany and a matching floppy blue one for herself.

While Lori browsed the hats and purses, Ramón secretly purchased a silver pendant for her. Though Ramón was laughing and joking during their excursion, he was actually dreading tomorrow, when he would have to say goodbye to Lori and watch her fly off into the clouds. She'd be alone in Houston and he'd be stuck in Acapulco without her. He had never felt so uneasy about letting a woman go, and this sense of dread settled on him like a heavy weight inside his chest.

After they returned to the yacht, the crew served them a late lunch of grilled snapper with fresh mango salsa on the promenade, as they sailed back toward the harbor.

After the yacht was safely back in port, Ramón thanked the captain and his crew for a fabulous day on the bay and told them they could leave.

Lori started toward the walkway, too, but Ramón held her back. "Not yet," he told her. "We're staying aboard."

"Oh, yeah?" Lori queried, assessing Ramón with a smile. "Why?"

"Come with me," he told her leading her from the upper deck back into the grand salon, where he popped the cork on a bottle of champagne and filled two crystal flutes.

Ramón handed a glass to Lori and then slipped a red box tied with white satin ribbon onto the granite bar.

"What's this?" she asked, eyeing him suspiciously.

"Something I picked up for you in the market today."

"When I wasn't watching," Lori commented.

"Absolutely. I wanted to give you something to remember this day," he hugged her to his side and kissed her on the lips, running his tongue lightly over her bottom lip.

"I don't need a gift to remember all of this," Lori replied, tilting her forehead to touch Ramón's while looking up at him through seductive eyes.

"Go ahead. Open it," he urged.

Lori quickly untied the satin ribbon and lifted the lid of the box. "Oh, my. This is beautiful," she remarked, holding up a silver chain with a heart-shaped pendant dangling from it.

"Like it?" Ramón asked, taking it from her to place it around her neck.

"I love it," Lori answered, tracing her fingers along the side of his face.

Ramón covered her hand with his and moved it onto his chest. "I love you, Lori," he told her, speaking each word slowly, carefully and with a hoarseness that betrayed his nervousness.

"I…I wish you wouldn't say that," she murmured.

When she tried to ease her hand out of his, Ramón held on tighter, refusing to release her. "Why? Do you think I'd say that if I didn't mean it?"

With a dip of her head, Lori paused, her lips pressed together in thought. "I believe you. It's just too soon for me to say how I feel. I don't know what's happening right now."

"I think you do, but you're just not ready to admit it."

"Maybe so," she agreed, sending Ramón an anguished glance

that told him how torn she was. "We're having a great time together, so let's not spoil it by making too much of a *commitment* so soon, okay?"

"Is that a dirty word as far as you're concerned?"

"No, not at all. But when I commit, it has to be permanent, and I don't want to make a foolish mistake."

Ramón reached out and ran his index finger over the curves of the silver heart around Lori's neck. "I hope you'll wear my gift as a sign of my commitment to you. I understand how you feel. I do. It's just that I want you to know that I'm yours. I'll wait." He kissed her on the forehead. "If I'm lucky, you'll come around."

Their lips met and held in a soft, loving way, sealing the decision to let their feelings play out over time while Lori adjusted to the impact of their fast-moving relationship.

"When we get back to Houston, I want you to meet my father," Ramón told Lori, having decided to move forward full speed, and pray that her feelings would catch up with his.

"Oh, Ramón. I don't know about that," she replied. "Meeting your father might imply that we're on our way to the altar, and that's not fair. Do you really want to do that right now?"

"Yes, I do. I'm very close to my father and I want to bring you into my life, Lori. He's a big part of it. You've already got my brother's stamp of approval and Carmen thinks you're the best thing that ever happened to me. I never dated that much. Never brought anyone home to meet my brother's family before, so he and Carmen already know you're very special to me."

"But maybe we'd be rushing it if I met your father. This thing in Acapulco just kind of happened."

"Aren't you glad it did?"

"Yes, I am," she replied, softening her tone. "I just don't want to give anyone the wrong impression," she said, assessing Ramón, watching for his reaction.

"The wrong impression?" Ramón stepped back, arms crossed on his chest, squinting at Lori in concern. "How?"

"All I meant, was… Oh, Ramón, I don't know how to say it. Guess I want to give whatever is happening between us some more time before I meet your father. I didn't have much of a choice as far as your brother was concerned, but your dad? That's another story."

Ramón reached out and placed both hands on Lori's shoulders, pinning her in place, forcing her to look at him. "I love you, and—" he guided her to the sofa and sat down on it beside her "—Lori, I know you love me, too."

"I can't say that."

"Why not? It's true. I've been thinking about this a lot. Maybe we…"

"We haven't known each other long enough to talk about love," Lori interrupted, determined to finish Ramón's sentence.

Ramón flinched, as if her words had slapped him hard. "How long we've known each other is not important. I knew the moment I saw you in the club that you were special, someone I wanted to get close to. Don't you know that love at first sight happens all the time?"

"Maybe in romance novels, rarely in real life," she countered.

"I disagree. My father married my mother only three days after they met, and he tells me all the time that I'll know when I meet the right woman. He's right. I know you're the woman for me."

Lori scooted to the edge of her seat and focused on the colorful carpet, avoiding looking at Ramón. "I care for you. I'm totally attracted to you and I love spending time with you, but I can't make more of a commitment than that. Don't rush me, please."

"Who's rushing? All I said was that I want you to meet my dad."

"Okay. I will, I promise. But when the time is right."

"And when do you think that will be?"

"Trust me. It'll all work out the way it's supposed to, if we don't try to force the issue. I made a huge mistake once before when I jumped into a relationship that should never have started. I really don't want to make plans or talk about commitment. Can't we just let things play out and see where we go?"

"Take a trip with no destination?" Ramón said. "That doesn't sound like a good way to travel. You fly the same route over and over when you're working. Maybe it's time for you to take off with no plan in mind. Who knows where you'll wind up or what will happen along the way? Give us a chance, okay?"

"A chance, sure. I want that, too," Lori relented as she looked over at him and smiled.

Ramón reached out to Lori and engulfed her in a bone-crushing hug. "Never doubt that I love you, Lori. However you want to play this out is fine with me, as long as we're together."

Lori let her body slump against Ramón's, her cheek pressed to his chest. As his heartbeat drummed in her ear, she held her breath, feeling fear for the first time since she'd met Ramón. Was she asking too much of him? Would her reluctance to commit drive him away? What if she blew it? And how could she go on if that happened?

Once they returned to the villa, Ramón went into his bedroom to shower and change, worried about how to proceed. How could he make Lori feel totally secure about his feelings for her? What did he have to do to convince her that he would never let her down? While standing under the shower, he bit his lip in concern. He had fallen hard for Lori. Very hard and very fast. He wanted more from her than she was willing to give. But any pressure would only scare her off.

"I've gotta play this cool," he reminded himself, aware that Lori's fears were perfectly understandable, even though he didn't share them. He would back off, give her all the space she wanted and show her that he could play the "no-strings attached" game, too. But taking that approach might push her further away instead of bringing her closer. Even so, it was a chance he had to take.

*The next day*

Lori zipped her flight bag, checked the bedroom to make sure she had all her belongings and then went out onto the veranda. Soon she would be departing for the airport. Her minivacation was over. It was time to get back to Houston and reenter the world she'd put out of her mind during this time alone with Ramón. Lori savored the spectacular view of Acapulco Bay one last time.

The white sand, the blue water, the constant fragrant breeze. "Paradise," she whispered, deciding to take a final walk along the beach.

Pulling on her new sun hat and Gucci shades, Lori set off along the shore of Xavier's private beach, enjoying the quiet of the morning. As the day wore on, the bay would come fully alive with boats, water skiers and parasailing tourists out for a fun-filled day. But right now, everything was calm and peaceful.

After walking a few yards from the house, Lori bent down to pick up a perfectly intact sand dollar that had washed up onto shore during the night. She brushed it off, admiring the bleached white color and distinctive markings of the fragile shell.

*A perfect souvenir,* she decided, encasing it in her palm and resuming her exploration of the shoreline. As she continued to scan the beach, her walk took her farther and farther from the house until she rounded a curve and came to a pile of driftwood that had been stacked along the shore. Lori bent to pick up a beautifully twisted branch, and then turned to continue her walk. However, she stumbled and gasped in surprise when a man in camouflage clothing walked out from behind a tall sago palm and stopped in her path.

"Oh!" Lori gasped, shocked as much by the man's unexpected appearance as by his size. He was huge, with square shoulders, a thick neck and arms that resembled sturdy brown saplings. She began to back up, thinking she must have strayed onto the neighbor's property. "I... I...didn't realize I'd come so far," she stammered, not knowing what else to say.

The man simply stood there, arms hanging on either side of his massive chest, reflective sunglasses hiding eyes that Lori knew were boring into her with great intensity.

"All right then. I'll just head on back to the house," she said, now in Spanish. He was clearly going to block her way and did not plan to let her venture any farther.

Not even a muscle moved in the man's face, letting Lori know that she was not going to have any kind of a conversation with him. Turning, she hurried back toward the house, puzzled by the encounter.

Approaching the house, she was relieved to see Ramón

walking toward her, waving. "We've got to go if you plan to make your flight," he called out, motioning for her to hurry up.

Lori waved back, increased her pace and caught up with Ramón

"I put your bag in the car," he said.

"Good, I'm all set. I just want to say goodbye to Carmen and Xavier."

"Okay, then let's go," Ramón said, taking Lori by the hand. "Have a good walk?"

"Yes, I did. But—" she hesitated, taking a deep breath "—did you see a man down there?" she asked, motioning toward the opposite end of the beach.

"A man? No. Why?"

"He was just there, near a huge pile of driftwood, looking at me really strangely. It was the creepiest thing." She gestured again far down the beach. "He came out of nowhere. A really nasty-looking man."

Ramón shrugged, seemingly unconcerned. "Probably one of Xavier's security people. Nothing to worry about. No strangers can get access to this private beach. He must belong here, and you were totally safe."

"I suppose so," Lori commented, taking one last look at the spot where the stranger had been before going inside to say her goodbyes to Xavier and Carmen.

The ride to the airport was bittersweet. Lori sat in silence and watched the ocean while Ramón focused on the winding highway leading away from the house. The tension between them was apparent, and Lori wasn't sure if it was because they were going to be separated for the next few days or because she had not been able to commit totally to Ramón. Even though she tried to relax, while telling herself everything would work out as she wanted, her heart was weighed down with worry.

When Ramón pulled up to the Passenger Dropoff at the airport and put the car in Park, she wanted to slide into his arms, profess her love, and recant her earlier remarks. But she couldn't do that.

Not yet. So when he kissed her goodbye and told her he loved her, all she could say was, "I'll miss you like crazy, and I'll be counting the days until you get home." She knew that was the truth.

## Chapter 16

"Haven't seen you in days. We gotta catch up," Brittany said, escorting Lori into the kitchen, where a plate of brownies awaited.

"I know," Lori said, settling in while Brittany poured two cups of espresso. "I had three trips back to back and then I volunteered to fill in for an attendant who couldn't make her New York run. I'm exhausted, but glad to be home for a few days."

"I guess so. Now what about Acapulco with Ramón's family? You never did tell me what went down. Was it really over the top?" Brittany pressed.

"Too fabulous to describe," Lori said, launching into a description of Xavier Vidal's family and his seaside estate.

"I've been to that area, and I think I know which house you're talking about. Villa Marquesa on Tropicana Road. Yeah, I partied at the house next door during my TV days. Some Mexican movie director owns it, though I don't exactly remember much about the place. I was rarely sober back then, you know?" Brittany admitted with a wry laugh, though her tone was matter-of-fact.

"I've never been in such a luxurious home," Lori said.

"Do Mexican judges make that kind of money?" Brittany probed, giving Lori a skeptical scowl.

Lori reached for one of the brownies Brittany had just taken from the oven, took a bite and then grinned. "Nobody makes brownies like you. That's why I wouldn't even try."

"They did turn out pretty good, didn't they?" Brittany admitted, sipping from her mug.

"In answer your question, Brit, no. Judges in Mexico don't make enough money to live the lifestyle that Xavier enjoys."

"But a lot of them and other law enforcement take bribes and money under the table."

"Not Xavier. He's completely honest…a man you can definitely trust," Lori said firmly. "From what Ramón told me, Xavier's wife, Carmen, comes from a wealthy family in Argentina. Her father makes sure she can live the good life without worry. Xavier adores his wife, and they have the most precious daughter, Linda. They seem like a very happy family. You know, I felt right at home with them…I like them a lot." Lori tucked one sandal-clad foot beneath her hips and leaned forward. "Ramón told me that their yacht was a…"

"Yacht?" Brittany interrupted, eyes wide in disbelief. "You gotta be kidding."

"Oh, noooo. It's called *La Princesa*. Ramón and I cruised Acapulco Bay on it. Fabulous. Too beautiful to imagine."

"Damn, girl, sounds like you hit the big time with Ramón."

"I don't know about that. He's not rich."

"Doesn't matter. He's got access, and believe me, that's all that matters."

"Umm, I have to disagree," Lori pushed back. "Money isn't everything."

"It damn sure comes close," Brittany quipped.

"Ramón does very well with his security business, but he's not like Xavier at all. He isn't caught up in appearances or extravagant living. He lives a fairly understated life in a condo near the senior center where his father lives."

"While Xavier and Carmen live like royalty down there on the bay?"

"Yeah, you could say that," Lori agreed. "Carmen is very

sweet, but I think she does like to flaunt her status as the wife of a prominent judge."

Brittany sat back in her chair and nodded. "Yeah, when I was on TV, I used to shop Rodeo Drive with a chauffeur to carry my packages. It was the good life, all right." She stopped, sputtered into laughter, and shook her head. "But I was usually so high I had no idea what I was buying or why." She paused for a beat while her words filled the silence. "Whew! Those were some days," she admitted, "and I am so glad I'm not there any more."

Lori watched her friend closely, unable to imagine Brittany in such a sad state, though she knew her neighbor was speaking the truth. The downfall, and recovery, of teen star Brittany Adams had made tabloid covers for months, and Lori had followed the sad saga with interest, never dreaming that she would live next door and become friends with the woman who'd so drastically changed her life. Not wanting to dwell on pain from the past, Lori quickly changed the subject.

"So, what's happening with the community-watch program?" she asked.

Brittany's face lit up and a huge grin curved her mouth. "Clint and I've been spending a lot of time together working on the project, so it's coming along."

Lori slapped her palm down on Brittany's glass-top table and squinted one eye closed in a suspicious gleam. "You are looking entirely too happy, Brit. Something more is going on with Detective Washington than the community-watch program. Something else you'd like to share?"

"Hmm. Not yet" was Brittany's cagey reply as she tented her fingertips and leaned across the kitchen table to zero in on Lori. "But maybe soon."

Lori licked her lips, clearly wanting more. "Come on. I told you all about my fun in the sun with Ramón in Acapulco. You owe me. Give it up, girlfriend."

"Okay, okay. He invited me to attend the police department banquet and dance on Saturday. At the Oaks Royal Country Club. Black tie. Live music. Our home girl, Beyoncé, is headlining."

"Of course, you said yes."

"Of course."

"Good for you! Sounds like you and Detective Washington are really hitting it off. Where do you see this going?" Lori probed, excited that Brittany had found a man she truly liked.

"Dunno. But when I do, you'll be the first to know," Brittany said.

"I'd better be," Lori tossed back. "After all, it was my crime scene that brought Clint Washington out here. You never would have met him if some crazy kids hadn't broken into my house and trashed it, so you've got me to thank if this turns into something special, okay?"

Brittany stood, went to her sink, placed her coffee cup into it, then turned and faced Lori. "You're right. Strange how things work out, huh?"

"Definitely," Lori agreed.

"So, when's your next trip out?"

"Tomorrow morning. Mexico City and back. No leg to Acapulco this time."

"How does Ramón take all your comings and goings?"

"We've decided that we can be together as much as possible between flights and not worry about the separations. It's my job, I love it and that's just the way it is."

"Do you ever think your job could cause problems? Remember what it did to you and Devan."

"Devan was crazy. He'd have complained if I were a saleslady at Macy's. He just wanted total control of my life and I wasn't about to buckle under his pressure. Ramón is so different. I think he kinda gets off on our goodbyes the night before I travel, as much as he anticipates my return. Our comings and goings make for some pretty intense encounters, if you know what I mean."

"I can just imagine," Brittany replied, fanning her face with her fingers.

"But, Ramón's got the travel bug, too," Lori added. "He's always talking about dream vacations…where we would go if we ever got our schedules to mesh."

"And where *would* you go if that ever happened?" Brittany asked.

"We finally decided that a month touring Brazil would be

the ultimate getaway. Rio is one place that Ramón is itching to visit."

"I can understand why." A beat. "Beautiful country. Beautiful people. And swimsuits are definitely optional at many of the beaches. You ready to go topless and mix with the locals?" Brittany teased with a laugh.

"I'll have to think about that," Lori tossed back at Brittany.

"Hey, I can picture you and Ramón strolling the beach, holding hands. Looking good. Exactly where two lovers ought to be."

"I think so, too," Lori replied, already visualizing the scene. The thought of being in a sexy, seductive locale like Rio with Ramón created a tingling sensation inside Lori that tickled her chest and flashed hotly between her legs. All she wanted at that moment was to make love to her man, and she could hardly wait until she saw him tonight.

## Chapter 17

Businesswise, things were looking up for Ramón. He and his partner, Keith, were doing well at Vida-Shield Security, scouting new accounts, working up contracts and supervising installations wherever their products were required. Traffic on the Vida-Shield Web site had increased threefold, allowing them to reach deeper into their consumer base to promote and sell all over the country. However, the majority of their accounts, both residential and commercial, remained in the greater Houston area—a sprawling geographic landscape with ever-present security needs.

Though Ramón wished it did, work alone couldn't fill the void left by Lori's frequent absences. And just when he'd thought she was going to be at home for a much-needed stretch, she agreed to fill in for a coworker on the New York-to-London flight. This last separation had been agonizing for Ramón, who could hardly wait for her late arrival tonight. He had the entire evening planned in detail. He'd texted Lori earlier and asked her to change from her GAA uniform into something casual as soon as she got to Houston, and to wait for him at Baggage Claim. He planned to whisk her off to an elegant dinner at the ZaZa to let her know how much he'd missed her.

When she was away, he tried not to think too much about what Lori was doing, with whom, and where. He'd understood from the beginning that Lori would always be on the go, and had convinced himself that it was no big deal—that her non-stop traveling wouldn't bother him. But it did.

He didn't worry about her safety on the plane. After all, flying was safer than driving across town. And he didn't worry about the physical and emotional demands of her job: she was prepared for any situation that might arise in flight or on the ground. However, Ramón fretted over all the free time she had on her hands once she hit the ground. She was thousands of miles away. On her own. And he knew Lori was not one to sit alone in her hotel room watching TV or reading a book. She loved to see the sights, meet new people, experience her environment and explore her surroundings. Wasn't that the way she'd found him?

So what, if she went out dancing or exploring the sights of London or New York? She didn't owe him any explanations. However, the thought of Lori dancing the night away in a smoky nightclub with a stranger sent a spiral of anxiety through Ramón, who had no interest in dancing with anyone other than her. Even though he occasionally went to a club or lounge, he preferred to go out for a beer or watch a game with his bachelor partner Keith whenever he wanted to get out.

Lori was beautiful, free-spirited and dead-set on living life as she pleased, and he had to admit that her outgoing personality was part of the reason he was attracted to her. Nothing clingy or oppressive about Lori. She played it cool and never made demands, but sometimes he wished she would. While in Acapulco, she had made it clear that she didn't plan to tie herself down with a serious commitment, but Ramón had no doubt that her feelings for him were stronger than she was willing to admit. It still surprised him how easily he'd allowed himself to become accustomed to Lori's presence, and when he thought back to life before he'd met her, he realized how monotonous and predictable his life had been. Now he wanted nothing more than a life of loving Lori.

*I'll bring her around to my way of thinking,* he vowed, smiling to himself as he pulled into the parking lot of the Old Mill Assisted Living Center, looking forward to his Father's Day evening out with his father.

"Tastes just like back home in Chilapa," Tomás Vidal said to his son, grinning as he wiped his mouth with a blue napkin. "*Enchiladas verdes* with tomatillo sauce. Nothing better than that for a Father's Day dinner on the town."

"But not as good as Mom's," Ramón noted, watching his father fold a warm tortilla in half and load it up with chili gravy and slices of avocado before taking a huge bite.

"Well, no one could beat your mother's cooking," Tomás said between chews. "I remember her *frijoles rojas, cabrito con maiz.* Ah…" Tomás sat back from the table and shook his head, allowing the piped in mariachi music to drift through the restaurant and fill in for the words he could not speak. Glancing at the ceiling, as if communing with his departed wife, he went on. "I used to tell your mother she shoulda opened a restaurant so the world coulda enjoyed her cooking, but she always told me, 'Tomás, I don't cook for money. I cook for love. For my boys. All of them, including you.'"

Tomás laughed under his breath and lowered his gaze. "And that's what she did until the end of her days with us. She loved her family, took good care of us and never complained, even though I knew how sick she was. She was a strong woman, your mother. I wish she were here right now, sitting in that empty chair, even though I know she'd be mad as hell to see me wearing denim. She hated jeans. Said they reminded her of the days before we came to America, when I was working in the fields from daybreak to dusk, trying to feed my family."

With a short incline of his head, Ramón told his father how well he understood. His thoughts wandered back to his deceased mother, something he tried not to do very often. His parents had been married for forty-five years when her sudden death from ovarian cancer took her away, devastating everyone who knew and loved her. She had been the force behind Ramón's drive to succeed, the one who'd pushed him to claim all that he could from this American way of life that she had struggled to embrace. His mother's death had been an unexpected blow that still reverberated through him like strange music from a harp; sometimes calming, sometimes jarring, but always playing just below the surface of his daily life.

"Your mother used to love to talk about what coming to America meant to her, and for her sons," Tomás continued, interrupting Ramón's inward musing. "To her, the most important thing in life was working hard and getting an education. We survived some rough times after we first arrived in Texas, but she never faltered in her belief that we'd made the right decision to become American citizens. Now I know she's bursting with pride to have one son a federal judge in Mexico, and the other making loads of money in business in America." A sigh of contentment escaped his lips. "You know what?"

"What?" Ramón asked, treasuring this time alone with his father.

"Your mother called you and Xavier a bridge between her two beloved homelands—Mexico and America. In her mind, they would never be separated. I'll bet she's smiling at you right now."

"I think you're right, Pop," Ramón agreed, aware that both he and his father had tears in their eyes and neither was ashamed to let them fall.

After leaving the restaurant, Ramón returned his father to Old Mill, happy to have been able to spend Father's Day with him.

Deciding to head across town to his office to finish some paperwork he'd let slide, Ramón swung onto the freeway. It was nine-thirty in the evening, so he would be able to concentrate without any interruptions. During the day, the phones were constantly ringing, his staff members were always asking him questions or he was giving them guidance. Though Ramón employed three full-time administrative staffers to oversee contracts, invoicing and billing, he never let a week go by without giving his books a thorough review.

After passing through his remote-controlled access gate, he parked his truck, popped the driver's side door open and stepped out. He clicked the remote, locked his vehicle and turned onto the walkway to the front entrance of the one-story building designed specifically for Vida-Shield. Instead of paying high rent for expensive office space, Ramón and Keith had taken the leap three years ago to construct their own building. The property was secure—surrounded by tall iron fencing and fitted with motion-sensor lights with tall streetlamps illuminating the front of the building.

Ramón reached into his shirt pocket and felt for the keycard he would need to open the front door.

Suddenly, he heard the harsh sound of metal scraping against metal and the tap of footsteps on asphalt. His head snapped up in alarm. Someone had forced the lock on the gate and was cutting across his private parking lot! Ramón stopped, more annoyed than concerned. He peered into the darkness, curious about who would be bold enough to damage his gate and trespass on his property.

When he saw two figures walking toward him in quick, hurried steps, he called out in a demanding tone, "Hey, what's going on? Who are you and what do you want?" In the split second that followed, he thought about the incident at Lori's house, aware that teen vandals were always roaming the city, spray paint cans in hand, out to do damage for kicks.

However, he quickly saw that the men headed toward him didn't look like teenagers dead-set on spray painting graffiti on his walls or skateboarding through his parking lot. He could not see their faces, but their silhouettes told him they were mature, stocky and dressed in dark trousers and white short-sleeved shirts with collars. And one of them was carrying a heavy crowbar.

When neither man responded to Ramón's demand to identify themselves, he lifted his chin, squared his shoulders and stepped forward, blocking the sidewalk by standing with his arms folded across his chest. Calmly, he waited for one of them to speak, but when they simply stopped a few feet away and glared at him, Ramón inched even closer. He sensed right away that they knew who he was. "I own this building. What do you want? Are you looking for me?" he demanded.

"As a matter of fact, we are," the taller of the two replied.

Ramón noticed that the one who spoke had badly pitted skin on the lower portion of his face, and the scarring created a craggy, evil appearance.

"So what do you want?" Ramón asked again, jaw jutted out in question.

Without another word, the man with the pitted face dropped the crowbar to the ground, and rushed forward, moving so swiftly that Ramón had no time to escape. His assailant grabbed Ramón by the shoulders and pushed him back against the chain-link fence that ran alongside the building.

Instinctively, Ramón kicked back, landing a hard blow inside the man's left thigh.

"Damn you, asshole!" the man screamed. He dug his fingers into the fleshy part of Ramón's collarbone and curled them down intensely.

Though the pain was excruciating, Ramón held his tongue, then managed to jerk his shoulder free and jam his elbow into the man's barrel-shaped chest.

A hard slap to the jaw was Ramón's reward.

"What the fuck do you want?" Ramón cursed, shocked by this aggressive attack. He made a hard fist with his right hand and shoved it into the face of the man's companion who suddenly came at him on the side. "Get outta here," Ramón shouted, swinging again, but missing this time. Scarface grabbed Ramón's arm, twisted it against his back and pinned him against the fence.

"What the hell is going on?" Ramón shouted, feeling the iron grids biting into his lip.

"Inside," the attacker growled.

*Only one thing to do,* Ramón decided. *Calm down. Try to defuse the situation before it gets even more out of control.* "Okay, okay. If you just tell me what you want, there'll be no more trouble."

"Shut up," the one who'd lagged behind hissed, his words cloaked in a thick Spanish accent.

Ramón jerked back his head, straightened his spine and clamped his mouth shut, knowing he'd inflamed the situation. Security was his profession. He knew the drill. *Stay calm. Give the perpetrators whatever they want and do not resist. Cooperate, unless they try to push me into a vehicle and take me from the scene.* "If it's money you're after," he boldly stated, trying to reach into his hip pocket, "here." He managed to grab hold of his wallet, which he tossed onto the strip of grass alongside the fence, hoping to distract one of the men and give him a chance to escape. He only had about $50 in cash in it and knew he could be beaten or killed because he wasn't carrying big bucks, but it was a chance he had to take.

"I said shut up!" the one with the accent growled at Ramón. He spun Ramón around, laughed aloud and then spit on the ground. "Be quiet if you wanna get outta here alive."

"Take the money. No more trouble. Okay?" Ramón lied, unable to keep quiet.

However, his offer of money initiated a hard blow across the mouth that sent him reeling backward, the hard edge of the fence cutting into his shoulder blades.

"Keep talking and you're dead," his scarred assailant warned, his voice much deeper, but with less of an accent. "I don't want your money."

"What *do* you want?" Ramón spat out, furious and seething with anger. Adrenaline coursed through him, making him eager to take these two on. He was in good shape and these men looked beefy, but not that fit. He could take them down if it came to that, and he was mad enough to try.

"Information." Scarface gave Ramón's jaw a hard slap.

Unable to let the slap pass, Ramón drove his fist into the man's belly, making him scream and double over, and then swung around to deliver a hard jab across the other man's neck.

Scarface recovered from the unexpected assault, grabbed Ramón by his shirtfront and yanked them nose to nose.

Ramón glared at the man as a warm, wet liquid ran down his chin and into his shirt collar. *Blood.* A throb of pain started up on the side of his face. Gritting his teeth, he held his breath, determined not to let them know how much pain he was in.

"What kind of information?" Ramón managed, squinting into the yellow light that shone down on them from the streetlamps at the curb. He could tell that they were Hispanic, and more mean-looking than he'd first realized. They looked like the type of actors who usually starred in B-rated gangster movies, with tattoos on their forearms and fake diamonds in their ears. Only these two were playing for keeps and there was nothing phony about the pain they were inflicting.

"You installed a security system in Xavier Vidal's house in Acapulco. I want the override codes to disarm the alarms."

With a snap, Ramón shook his head back and forth, stunned to realize that the men who were out to ruin his brother had now turned their scare tactics on him. Lopez's threat may have reached him in Houston, but Ramón was not going to give up any information that would put his brother in danger.

Another jarring punch landed on Ramón's jaw. He winced, braced himself against the pain, and then spat a glob of blood onto the sidewalk. Chest heaving, he narrowed his eyes at the taller man, who suddenly pulled a gun from beneath his shirt and pointed it at Ramón.

"Don't make me use this," he warned in a gravelly voice, pressing the snub-nose revolver into Ramón's chest.

Though the pain in his jaw was growing more intense and his insides felt like scrambled eggs, Ramón knew he had to hold it together and summon help somehow. "Okay, okay," he muttered, pretending to give in. "Inside. I have the information you want in my office."

"Good. That's better," the gunman grunted, relaxing his grip on Ramón.

Shaking off the two men, Ramón led them toward the front of his building, taking bold, strong steps as his mind spun ahead to come up with a plan. He suddenly knew what he had to do to escape without getting shot. It was chancy, but he was willing to take the risk.

Motion-sensor lights snapped on as soon as the trio stepped up to the door, illuminating the entire front of the building.

"Shit! Hurry up!" the gunman ordered, poking Ramón with his weapon. "Open the goddamn door and get outta this light!"

Ramón took out his keycard, bent over and pretended to slip it into the slot while praying his plan would work. Bracing his head against the frosted glass insert in the door, he fumbled with the keycard, aware that the pressure he was putting on the glass was sending a silent alarm to alert the police that someone was trying to enter the building who did not have a keycard.

"Quit stallin'. Open the fuckin' door and get in there," the one with the heavily accented voice commanded, one hand on Ramón's back, pushing him even harder against the glass. "You gonna give us what we need to get into the judge's safe, and you're gonna make sure he cooperates."

"Why should I?" Ramón blurted out, groping to buy time, certain the police were on their way. When he'd designed his building, he'd wired the silent alarm system into the glass part of the door, never dreaming he'd be the first one to try it out. He shifted his lower jaw from side to side, testing his ability to move it.

"Damn, I think you broke my jaw," he accused, just as another pain shot upward into his temple, burning a white-hot path through his head.

"I'm gonna break more than that if you don't hurry up," the assailant growled. "Go on. Open the damn door!"

The scream of a police siren was music to Ramón's ears. Tensing, he knew the men would either flee in fear or shoot him to keep him from talking to the authorities. Maybe both? *But why would they do that?* he thought, analyzing the situation and hyped up on adrenaline. *If they want information that only I can give them, they won't take me down. Will they?*

The pulsating siren grew louder and closer. Ramón clenched his teeth and squinted hard at the men, who seemed confused about what move to make.

"You'd better take off while you still have time," Ramón taunted, doubting they would shoot him before running away.

Pivoting away from Ramón, the one who seemed to be in charge, or at least the one who had been doing most of the talking, took off, leaving Ramón standing in the entryway.

"We *will* get what we want, one way or another. If you don't want more trouble, you'll cooperate," the other man warned, lifting a menacing finger to Ramón's face. "And so will your brother." Then he ran across the parking lot and out the damaged gate.

The shock of the encounter left Ramón outraged, and fearful for Xavier and his brother's family. These men were obviously working for Aldo Lopez and they would stop at nothing to get what they were after.

*And I won't stop until I get revenge for this vicious attack,* Ramón vowed, clenching his fists as the wailing police car pulled through the gate and headed toward the building.

# Chapter 18

The officers who responded to Ramón's silent alarm immediately sent out an APB alert to patrol cars in the area to find the men who attacked Ramón. They also called for an ambulance to take Ramón to the emergency room, and when the police officer in charge asked Ramón whom he should contact to meet him at the hospital, his answer was "No one."

The fact that there was nobody he could summon to be with him created an empty feeling that settled in Ramón's stomach like a rock sinking in deep water. No way would he burden his elderly father with this kind of frightening news and he didn't dare drag his partner, Keith, into the situation because there'd be too much explaining to do. Besides, Ramón had promised Xavier that he wouldn't tell anyone about the problem in Mexico, so he had no option other than to keep mum and hope for the best. This was Ramón's problem to solve, and he'd have to do it without involving anyone close to him, especially not Lori.

As the ambulance raced along the freeway, lights whirling, siren screaming, Ramón's thoughts remained on Lori. Her plane was set to land in less than an hour and here he was, lying on a gurney on his way to the hospital instead of at the airport clutching a bouquet of roses and waiting to welcome her home. He reached down to his waist and felt for his cell phone, which he usually clipped to his belt. Even though he had no idea what he planned to tell Lori, he knew he had to call and let her know why he would not be there as he'd told her he would. When his hand swept over his belt, he realized that his phone was in his truck, which was still in the parking lot outside his building.

"Dammit!" Ramón muttered. This was not how he'd expected his evening to turn out, and he was not feeling good about the situation at all.

With three stitches in his bottom lip and a prescription for pain medication in his hand, Ramón made his way through the hospital corridors to a bank of pay phone cubicles near the cafeteria, where he immediately telephoned Xavier. When Carmen came on the line, sounding as if he'd awakened her, she informed Ramón that his brother was in Mexico City for a hearing on an important case.

"When will he be back?" Ramón asked.

"Not until late tomorrow," Carmen replied. "Is it important? I can give you the number to his hotel."

"Naw. I don't want to bother him this late," Ramón said, deciding not to disturb Xavier the night before his hearing. He knew his brother well. Once he was awakened, Xavier never could go back to sleep, and there was nothing he could do about Lopez tonight anyway. "I'll call him in the morning."

"Call early, if you want to get him," Carmen advised. "He'll leave the hotel very early and he never carries his cell phone into court, so once he's out of the hotel, he's kinda out of touch. But you can always leave a message with the court clerk for him to call you when he's free."

"Uh…thanks, I will." Ramón studied the white tile squares on the hospital floor as he considered the situation. "Are you and Linda okay?" Ramón probed, hoping nothing had happened to Carmen or her daughter while Xavier was away.

"Sure. We're fine." The phone went silent for a brief pause

before Carmen went on. "Why? You sound kinda strange. You worried about something?"

"Naw. Just want to make sure you girls are okay." Ramón sagged against the metal frame that surrounded the phone cubicle and propped his throbbing chin on one hand. "I'll check with Xavier tomorrow."

After disconnecting the call, Ramón leaned against the side wall of the cubicle and closed his eyes. The strain of the evening was fast taking its toll on him. He was dead tired, hungry and more pissed off than alarmed over being attacked. He had no idea about how to make it happen, but one thing was certain: Lopez was going down.

It had been a long, exhausting day and right then all he wanted to do was go home, fall into bed and sleep for the next twenty-four hours. But he knew he couldn't do that. Obviously, if Lopez's men knew so much about his movements, then they must also know about Lori. He had to get to Lori, make sure she was okay and do everything in his power to keep her safe—without making her aware of the danger she was in.

# Chapter 19

Lori disarmed her new security alarm, dropped her flight bag and kicked off her shoes. God, she was glad to be home! Seemed like this trip had lasted forever. And what had happened to Ramón? He'd been so specific in his instructions. Why didn't he show up?

*Maybe his father needed him,* she decided, flicking off the porch light that she'd left burning while she was gone.

When her cell phone rang, she took it out of her purse and checked the screen. She nodded. Just as she suspected, it was Ramón. With a jab of her index finger, she took the call, annoyed, frustrated and curious about what had happened to him.

"Hello," she said, deliberately using a cool and distant tone to let him know from the get-go that she was not happy about being abandoned at the airport. Sliding onto a barstool at her kitchen counter, she rested her chin on a fisted hand and squinted at nothing in particular. *This had better be good,* she thought, drawing in a steady breath.

"Finally! I got you!" Ramón called out, sounding relieved.

"I wasn't lost," she tossed back with a snap. "So where are you, anyway?"

"On my way to your house."

"Really? Why? Did I miss something? Weren't you supposed to meet me at Baggage Claim?"

"Yeah, but something happened that threw everything off."

"You coulda called. I changed my clothes and was there on time, waiting for you, ready to go."

"I know. That was the plan, but I had to deal with something that couldn't wait. I'll tell you all about it when I get there," Ramón hurried to explain, speaking so fast that Lori could hardly make out what he was trying to tell her.

She frowned and was quiet long enough to convey her mood, which was far from the way she wanted to feel. She had certainly expected a better explanation about his absence. After all, the whole change-clothes-and-wait-for-me arrangement had been Ramón's idea, and she had been willing to go along with him, even though that was not what she'd wanted to do. She would have preferred to go home, wind down in a steamy bubble bath and pull herself together before heading out. Now she was irritated, starving and more than a little pissed that he'd left her standing at Baggage Claim, looking and feeling like a fool. To be stood up at the airport had been a humiliating experience.

"Something came up?" Lori snapped, wanting to know more. She'd waited nearly an hour before deciding to head home and was not in the mood to play guessing games with him. What she really wanted was to be left alone tonight to enjoy some peace and quiet. "I think I deserve something better than that. I called your cell four times. Didn't you get my messages? And why didn't you answer your phone?"

"Got separated from my phone, but I have it now. Sorry about that."

"Yeah? So, what's been going on with you?" Lori wanted to know, beginning to feel anxious. Was he backing away from her? Had her fear of commitment pushed him too far away? A small voice inside her head told her she didn't want to hear the truth while another voice demanded to know all.

"As I said, I'll tell you everything when I get there. Promise," Ramón replied.

"All right. Later," Lori conceded, clicking off before he could say another word.

Exasperated as much with herself as with Ramón, she wished she'd told him to forget about getting together tonight. But since he was already headed to her house, she might as well get ready to go out.

Passing through her front entry, she stopped in the foyer to pick up a stack of envelopes and papers that the mail carrier had shoved through the mail slot in her door. In her bedroom, she flipped on the ceiling fan to freshen up the room and casually began to sort through the jumble of envelopes, circulars and cards that had arrived while she was away. An electric bill, her renewed American Express card, a reminder from her dentist that it was time for her annual checkup, a few pieces of junk mail and an ivory-colored envelope with her name and address handwritten on the front. It had no return address, but it had been postmarked in Houston.

She didn't recognize the handwriting, but something about it gave her pause. The scrawl was tiny, ragged and uneven, as if written by a child. Curious, Lori sat down on the side of her bed, tore open the envelope and glanced, first, at the signature before reading the letter. With a snap, her eyes widened and her jaw dropped.

"Oh, no," she groaned. "This can't be happening. What is this about?"

The letter was from Devan Parker! After all this time, how dare he intrude on her life now? She sure didn't need this kind of a shock on top of Ramón's mysterious absence, which had left her disappointed and shaken.

Gently, Lori unfolded the single sheet of paper. She held it by the corners—as if it might contain some dangerous powder or contaminant that he had placed inside. Tensing, she traced the tightly scripted words with suspicious eyes, her heart racing as she read:

*Dear Lori,*
*I know you're surprised to hear from me, as I promised*
*never to contact you again. I know I made a complete mess*

*of things with you, but I hope you'll read my letter and not feel threatened by this effort on my part to let you know what has happened to me.*

*I owe you so much. You saved my life. If you had not broken off our relationship and insisted I get professional help, I know I would have self-destructed by now. How could I have been so stupid? Why didn't I see that the way I was expressing my love for you was driving you away rather than bringing us together? For a long time now, I've been in therapy, dealing with what my doctor says are deep-seated feelings of insecurity, which according to him caused manic/depressive behavior. Anyway, that's why he says I tried to hold on to you so tightly that I pushed you away.*

*This therapy thing has been a painful, eye-opening experience, but it's helped me learn how to control my emotions. I've learned to appreciate myself and value relationships without smothering the people I love. Because you went to court and got a restraining order on me, you forced me to deal with my problems and take a hard look at myself. I want you to know that I am a different man now. I understand—for the first time in my life, that loving someone does not mean possessing them. I have to give you all the credit for this miraculous turnaround, Lori. I just hope that one day you will forgive me for all the trouble I caused you. You deserve to be treated with respect and appreciation, not controlled and possessed. You are a class act, Lori, and I'll love you forever.*
*Devan.*

Lori rested on her elbows and watched the ceiling fan throw dark shadows across her pale peach bedroom walls. The oblong shapes shifted and blended into curious forms as they moved down the walls, mimicking the swirl of emotions racing through Lori. Devan's unexpected letter both shocked and pleased her, spawning a torrent of memories that she could not keep from flooding back just when she'd thought her chaotic involvement with him was forever in her past.

Devan had been handsome, charismatic, full of energy and excitement. He'd swept her off her feet when they first met, but dropped her with a crash at the end. Thinking back, she knew his erratic behavior had been rather manic, and his mood swings had been difficult to deal with. But between the highs and lows, she'd continually forgiven him for his over-the-top possessiveness, thinking that things would change in time. However, loving Devan had been a roller-coaster ride of laughter, followed by tears, with both of them refusing to face the fact that what they had was a lopsided relationship with no staying power. However, Lori knew she'd held on too long, intensifying Devan's connection to her while making the final separation more difficult.

*How strange,* she thought, letting Devan's stunning confession sink in. *He's thanking me for saving his life!* As upsetting as their breakup had been, she was proud of Devan for taking charge of his problems. Seeking professional help must have been hard for him to do and, yet, he'd been brave enough to face the truth and deal with it. A warm feeling came over Lori to think that she might have played a part in helping Devan overcome his emotional troubles and move on with his life.

With a shudder, Lori sat up and sighed. *Why was I so desperate to make things work with him?* she now wondered. "Well, it's finally over," Lori admitted, relieved to know that Devan was in a better place emotionally and doing well. She had never wished him ill, only wished him to go away, and now his letter had brought much-needed closure to their relationship.

Lori folded Devan's letter in half, tore it into tiny pieces, went into the bathroom and flushed it down the toilet, feeling as if a great weight had been lifted off her chest.

The chime of her doorbell pulled Lori out of the somber mood created by Devan's astonishing letter.

"Now, Ramón and his excuses," she muttered, wondering what was going on with him, and thinking that maybe she didn't even want to know.

However, one look at Ramón's swollen, bandaged lower lip and his badly bruised cheek banished all of Lori's earlier anger.

With a shocked gasp, she swallowed the zinger she'd planned to hurl at him, wishing she hadn't been so short-tempered on the phone.

Stepping back from the open door, she narrowed her eyes at Ramón, both alarmed and confused by his mangled appearance.

"Ohmigod! Were you in a car accident?" she guessed, taking his arm as she urged him inside.

"No, thankfully. I wasn't in a car wreck, but something just as bad went down," he replied, turning to face her as she closed the door.

"You've been to the hospital?"

He nodded. "The emergency room."

"But you're okay?"

Another nod. "The doc stitched up my lip, gave me a bottle of painkillers and released me. So all I need now is some tender loving care." He cocked his head to one side and gave Lori a sorrowful look, as if pleading for her to feel sorry for him. "However, no kissing until the swelling goes down and my lip returns to normal. Think you can wait that long?" He ran his tongue over his upper lip and then adopted a pouty expression.

"Stop joking, Ramón," Lori ordered, not seeing the humor in the situation. "This looks serious. How'd this happen and why didn't you call me? Did it happen while you were on a job?" she probed, aware that installing security systems could involve quite a bit of construction. Ramón had told her stories of near misses when walls had caved in or beams had fallen down while working on a complex installation.

"No. I didn't get hit by a two-by-four or a stray nail. I got mugged."

"Shit! Where? Oh, no. Come on. Sit down," Lori urged, guiding Ramón into the den and over to the sofa where he sat down while she remained standing over him. Lori examined his face, her heart racing as she realized how badly he'd been hurt. "Okay. Enough with the guessing. Spill it! What happened?" Her voice was high-pitched and tight with concern.

Instead of answering, Ramón reached up, pulled Lori down beside him and wrapped her in his arms. Cuddling her in a protective manner, he sighed, letting her know how relieved he was to finally have her next to him. With one hand pressed to the side of her head, he nudged her cheek against his neck, stirred by his need to have her near. She could feel the beat of his heart as it pounded at his throat, and when he drew in two more deep breaths, her body moved with his, rising and falling in silence as he took a moment to pull himself together.

"I was assaulted in the parking lot outside my building," he finally told her, easing back to look into her face.

"Did you call the police?" Lori gasped in alarm, rising up. She tried to pull out of Ramón's embrace, but he tightened his grip, as if afraid to let her go.

"Please. Don't move," he said, sounding weary. "I'm still shaken by all this. I just want to sit here and hold onto you for a minute. It's been a hell of a night. Like a really bad dream. Two men came out of nowhere. Slapped me around. One held a gun on me while the other kept jabbing me in the face. It hurt like hell."

Lori stilled in his arms, shocked by the thought that someone had tried to kill Ramón. Snuggling against him, she said a silent prayer of thanks that he was all right, never having felt so shaken in her life, and knowing she had to remain calm for him.

"Did they take your wallet?" she asked, looking up at Ramón.

"No. The cops arrived and scared them off before they were able to rob me."

"Damn," Lori murmured, holding onto Ramón's hand, uneasy about what he'd just told her. "But why were you at your office so late? You told me you were having a late dinner with your father."

"I did. But after I dropped him off, I decided to swing by the office and kill some time before I met you at the airport," he went on, speaking in a halting manner. "As soon as I got out of my truck, two men rushed me, but I managed to trip a silent alarm. The cops came right away and scared them off."

"Did you get a good look at them?"

"Not really. I gave the police the best description I could, but it was dark and the dim streetlights didn't help much."

"Hopefully, the police are after them now."

"I guess so. Anyway, as far as I'm concerned, it's all over."

"Yeah...thank God," Lori breathed, feeling ashamed of herself for acting so selfishly about Ramón's failure to meet her at the airport. At least he hadn't been seriously hurt. However, she had a sense that Ramón was deliberately downplaying the incident and wondered why. His cavalier attitude made Lori a bit annoyed. Why would he take such a casual attitude toward this assault when he was in the business of protecting other people?

"How do you feel?" she asked, running a hand along his bare arm, trying to get him to relax. What he needed from her was comfort, not criticism, and to know that she was there for him.

Ramón broke into a laugh as he touched a finger to his jaw. "If you really wanna know...I'm hungry as hell. I kinda picked over dinner with Dad, because I knew we were going out later."

Lori clucked her tongue in disapproval and scowled at Ramón. "Well, we're not going out now." She tugged on his hand. "Let's check out what I have in the kitchen. I'm starving, too, so I guess I'd better fix us something to eat," she confessed, slipping her arm around his waist as they headed toward the rear of the house. In the kitchen, she opened the freezer and removed two grilled chicken fillets, which she popped into the microwave to thaw.

"Keep talking. That'll keep your mind off the pain. Tell me about your dinner with your dad," she urged, eager to change the subject and take care of him. No way was she going to let Ramón get behind the wheel of his truck tonight. He'd been through quite a shock and now it was up to her to protect him. "You're spending the night here," she decided, knowing how men could be such little boys at times like this, loving all the attention. Besides, she liked being in the protective mode with her man. All of a sudden, his importance in her life took on new meaning and she knew that losing him would be unimaginable!

# Chapter 20

Ramón awoke the next morning with lingering effects of the assault and the stress from the day before. But what he also felt was Lori's perfectly shaped butt pressing against his stomach and a stiff hard-on that made him groan. He opened one eye, squinted into the strip of sunlight beaming into Lori's bedroom and thought back over the night before. He remembered eating grilled chicken and vegetables while sitting at the kitchen table, Lori's tender ministrations as she changed the bandage on his wound and her silky arms embracing him as he fell asleep.

Ramón also recalled that Lori's neighbor, Brittany, had dropped by, accompanied by Detective Washington. Ramón had told them about his attack, but refused the detective's offer to check into the case. No need to get any more people involved. He and Xavier would need to talk, make a plan and get this situation under control.

Lori stirred, yawned and rubbed her rear end back and forth against his swollen penis as she settled even closer. Ramón clenched his teeth in torment as a devilish grin played over his lips. He loved the way her sleek body fit with his, as well as the fact that his lip was no longer throbbing and his stress level was way down. In fact, he had never felt this content in his life. All because of Lori.

Scooting up to mold himself against her, Ramón trailed his tongue over the back of Lori's neck. His move initiated a shift of her body that pushed her hips flat against his well-primed member, which was standing at attention and eager for action. He spooned his knees beneath hers, fitting his legs into the hollow behind her thighs to rest his cheek onto her shoulder. Relaxing, he luxuriated in the exquisite rush of happiness that flowed through him. He was blissful. Satisfied with his life. And lucky to have a woman like Lori to love. With a sigh, he wrapped both arms around her body and hugged her hard, letting her know how much he adored her.

When Lori reached back with one hand and claimed his arousal, Ramón tensed. He hissed into her ear, "Watch out. My lip may be bruised and out of commission, but what you're holding onto is in perfect working condition."

"Hmm, I sure hope so," Lori whispered, massaging his warm shaft with a touch that made Ramón clamp his teeth together and pray for restraint. His entire body was on fire, hot with the need and a surging desire to totally possess Lori in a way he'd never done before. He slid his palm beneath her sheer nightgown and groped for the elastic edge of her panties, but was pleasantly surprised to find that she wasn't wearing any. Snaking his fingers into her pubic hair, he raked the soft patch with tender strokes, teasing her clitoris with a rapid back-and-forth movement that brought a raw moan from low in her throat. With a tilt of her spine, Lori arched her back and spread her thighs, allowing Ramón to take advantage of the opening and plunge two fingers deep inside her sensuous and slippery core, tantalizing her even further.

Taking care not to further injure his stitched-up lip, he used his tongue to trace slow, languid licks across the slope of Lori's bare shoulder, onto the tender flesh at the nape of her neck and into the soft spot behind her ear, loving the taste of her perfumed skin. An instant jolt of longing passed through him when she murmured, "Ah, that feels so good. Don't you dare stop." Her effortless expression of satisfaction intensified his emotional connection, making him even hornier than when he first woke up.

Lori's swift-moving fingers maintained control over his rock-hard shaft as she slid around to face him. With puckered lips, she placed three short kisses on the uninjured side of his mouth before sliding her tongue over each of his nipples and then down the center of his chest.

"Damn, baby, go right ahead," Ramón moaned when her lips claimed his erection. He made an upward thrust of his hips, pushing himself fully into her mouth while looking down onto the top of her head which was buried in the dark triangle between his legs. Her hand job had primed him to such a point that Ramón's temptation to let go was intensifying to an agonizing level. With her lips, teeth and tongue, she sucked and tugged and licked and squeezed his tool with an expert touch, providing just the right amount of pressure, countered by relief, as she stimulated him beyond imagination. Just when she'd sent him to the edge of a thundering climax, she brought him down by pulling away and blowing a stream of cool air onto his flaming flesh. He loved this erotic side of her! Her sexy moves and seductive manipulations had him hooked. She was the woman he would never tire of loving, and even though she literally had him by the balls, he was not complaining.

*This feels so damn good,* he silently mused, loving Lori's ability to sense what he wanted, and deliver. Her attention to his needs confirmed his belief that what they'd found together was very special, completely natural and meant to last. He'd waited a long time to find a woman like Lori, a woman who made him feel like a true partner in love, and now that he'd found her, he planned to do everything in his power to please her, satisfy her and love her forever.

As Lori's sizzling manipulation of his manhood increased, Ramón's sense of urgency did, too. Though he refused to give in and ruin their erotic ride, he did allow her to bring him to the point of imminent release once more while tamping down his impending eruption, balancing on the edge.

Gently, he cupped his hand beneath her chin and urged her

to release him. As he guided her upward, he smiled, looking forward to satisfying her sexual needs.

Ramón guided Lori onto him, and spread her knees on either side, making a slow, teasing sweep of his hands between her thighs as she settled down and accepted his easy penetration. While facing her, he used the fingers of one hand to fondle her slippery bud while the other tugged her nightgown over her head and flung it to floor.

Looking up into her face, he melted under her tender caress of a gaze as she studied him through eyes lit with fire—charged with the seductive energy of their intimate connection. Like a tiger that had captured its prey, she peered down at him through languid, hungry eyes—half-closed, yet gleaming with an intensity that told him he was doing exactly what she needed, wanted and expected.

Ramón's heart did a flip when Lori bent low, clamped her hands around his neck and pulled his mouth even with hers. Hovering just above her full, plump lips, he was dying to crush his mouth over hers, and his inability to kiss her as he wanted to only increased his desire to possess her completely. Like forbidden fruit, her luscious lips tempted him, enticed him and heightened his drive to find other ways to love her.

"Gotta go easy on the kisses," he reminded her in a voice heavy with longing.

"Kisses, I don't need," she seductively replied, wiggling her body, pushing his rigid member deeper between her legs.

Holding on to Lori, Ramón flipped her over onto her back and used both hands to raise her hips off the bed, driving into her with firm, urgent thrusts.

Lori threw back her head and claimed his shaft with her wetness, pushing him into her tunnel of love with soft grunts of satisfaction. "This is all I want," she told him, anchoring her legs around his waist, delighting in the physical bond that was holding them together.

Ramón pumped steadily, moving in and out, delivering slow, easy strokes that helped him gain control of his emotions while building momentum to go the distance. He placed one hand over each of her breasts and thumbed her nipples with tingling, circular movements, feeling them grow firm beneath his touch. Back and forth, round and round, he played a rhythmic number with his hands while delighting in the quivering outbursts of low tender moans coming from her lips.

Reciprocating his attention, Lori flattened her palms on Ramón's chest and ran her fingers through the fine mat of hair covering his upper body like soft silk. When she tweaked one of his nipples with a hard, playful pinch, he broke his stride long enough to give her a playful nip of a kiss on the nose, even though doing it made him wince.

Surrendering to her vibrating need, Ramón slid his hands off Lori's heavy breasts and pressed them along the firm plane of her stomach, drifting his touch along her thighs before he rocked her upward and brought her to her knees. Without withdrawing from her love-slick core, he rested her buttocks on his upper thighs, helping her create a viselike clench that fused them even more tightly than before. Yielding to the bursting sensation of uncontrollable joy, he moved into her with faster thrusts as his need for release surged higher.

"Give it to me! Give it all to me," Lori gasped, rocking back and forth.

"It's all yours," Ramón replied, shuddering in unspoken passion as a tremor of ecstasy slid through him, pushing him into the raging fire of seduction that was burning hotly inside.

Lori lifted her chin and swayed backward, arching her back and presenting luscious nipples that begged for his attention. Lowering his head, Ramón took a pointed nipple deep into his mouth and suckled it until she released a pleasure-filled cry. He captured the other one, teasing her unmercifully as he worked to bring her to that magic point of indescribable pleasure. Lori took his hand and plunged it down between her legs, pushing his fingers toward the throbbing center of her sex. First, he fondled it carefully, to make sure he was on target, then he twirled it in a tease, rubbing back and forth until he brought her to a searing climax that sent a cry of agonizing delight from her throat.

As Lori soared into her spiraling climb toward release, Ramón eased her down on the bed. With his body molded to hers, he let go of all restraint and allowed their erotic journey to peak in tandem.

Arriving simultaneously at their final destination melded Lori and Ramón into a shuddering embrace as they held on to each other and drifted to a perfect landing.

# Chapter 21

Lori remained in bed while Ramón went into the bathroom and turned on the shower. While recovering from the greatest sex she'd ever had, she luxuriated in the aftermath of the experience.

Damn, he sure as hell knew how to please her and didn't hold back at all. After having been mugged the night before, she'd hardly thought he'd be in the mood to do anything as incredible as what he'd just done with her.

"Hmm," she murmured, snuggling deeper into the tangled sheets that still held the scent of their sexual adventure. The smell of him made her suck in a breath and squeeze her legs together, prolonging the effect he'd had on her. Her body was still tingly and raw from his intense penetration, but the lingering sensation only made her want him more. *Another round when he returned? How could we possibly top what just happened?* she silently questioned, suppressing a light giggle with the back of her hand, doubting she could ever get enough of Ramón. Closing her eyes, she sighed. Perfect. That's what he was. The perfect man for her.

When Ramón emerged from the shower, drying his hair and with a towel around his waist, she eyed him with appreciation. He was gorgeous, but in addition to his drop-dead good looks, he was tenderly appreciative of her and her needs. He never pressured her or made demands, even though she knew he wanted more than she was willing to give. However, he was quickly wearing her down.

*Am I taking a risk by not deepening the relationship? Or am I doing the right thing by going slow?* Lori worried, determined to avoid the kind of heartache that she'd endured after her affair with Devan. She couldn't imagine going through that kind of turmoil again. Recovering from her last relationship had been too traumatic to repeat. All she wanted to do was enjoy Ramón, and he was certainly giving her a lot to be happy about.

"How's your lip? The rest of your body?" she asked, sitting up in the middle of the bed to beckon Ramón nearer.

"Much better. No pain at all. In fact, I feel like I could go another round with you, if you're game," he replied, sliding down onto the bed to brush her forehead with his nose.

She slapped him playfully on the arm, reached out and then slid her palm against his cheek, studying his stitched lip. "It looks pretty good. The swelling's gone down."

"Right. It'll be back to normal by tonight…so watch out. When I return, I'm gonna make up for lost time, so get ready to be kissed…a lot." He pulled on his shirt, and then paused to bend down and trace a finger over the space between Lori's naked breasts.

She curved her shoulders back and offered him better access, giggling when he leaned in and flicked his tongue over her beckoning nipples.

"Sweet. Too sweet. Please, don't tempt me," he mocked in agony, using a husky voice. Pulling way, he moved his head from side to side, as if admitting defeat. "Have you decided what you want to do for your birthday?" he asked.

"How did you know I had a birthday coming up?"

"Brittany caught me when I was leaving last time I was here and gave me a heads up."

"Sounds like her. Well, how does an overnight in San Antonio sound? We could book a suite at the River Walk Hilton. Have dinner on the balcony overlooking the river. Just hang out and act like regular tourists. What do you think?"

"Sounds *very* romantic," he replied. "Let me take care of everything, okay?"

"Fine with me," Lori replied.

Ramón gave her perky breasts a final caress and then moved away. "You'd better get dressed or we're going to be in trouble," he warned, giving her a look that contained a dare.

"Okay…I'm gone," Lori said with a flip as she jumped up from the bed and headed toward the bathroom. She paused at the door and looked back at Ramón, whose eyes remained fastened on her. "I won't be long," she added. "So don't you dare leave."

"Wouldn't think of it," he said as he strapped on his watch. "Want me to make coffee?"

"That would be wonderful," Lori replied, turning around, making sure Ramón got a damn good view of her naked butt as she walked away.

As soon as he'd put the coffee on, Ramón's cell phone rang. He checked the screen and saw that it was Xavier, so he answered right away.

"Carmen said you called last night. What's up?" Xavier asked.

"You really don't want to know," Ramón replied, lowering his voice to a whisper as he told Xavier about the incident with the two men who assaulted him.

"Yes, Lopez's boys got to me," Ramón repeated, going on to describe the men who'd attacked him. "The police are looking for them but they're probably on their way back to Mexico right now, so I doubt the authorities will catch them."

"Probably right," Xavier agreed. "Lopez is in the business of moving people across the border, so it doesn't surprise me that he'd send his thugs to Houston to intimidate you. Ramón, this is not good. I feel so bad about what happened. Are you sure you're okay?" Xavier pressed, sounding concerned.

"Three stitches in a busted bottom lip, some ugly bruises on my body, but no broken bones," Ramón told his brother. "I'm a pretty tough guy, you know? You don't have to worry about me. I want you to watch out for yourself and your family."

"I will, but I'm still worried about you. I can't believe how complicated and dangerous this whole situation has become. Damn! I'm sorry. I never should have gotten you involved."

"Hey, you needed security, that's what I do. We'll work through this. Don't worry. What I need from you is everything you can tell me about how these guys operate down there, so I can try to put some roadblocks in place."

"I hate to pull you deeper into this mess, Ramón. These men can be dangerous. No conscience at all," Xavier cautioned.

"Who else can you trust to help you deal with this besides me, huh?" Ramón threw back.

"No one, and that's the sorry truth, bro."

"All right then. Stop apologizing and let's make a plan to keep everyone safe until this thing is over," Ramón decided.

"We've gotta be vigilant and cautious," Xavier advised.

"But for how long?" Ramón asked, beginning to feel a bit impatient and irritated with his brother. This situation called for action. When he'd agreed to install a high-tech security system in Xavier's home, all Ramón had assumed he was doing was protecting his brother and his family. Now, he shuddered to think of how complicated this had become. His work had made him a target, too. Time was of the essence and there was not a minute to waste.

"What are the local authorities doing? Where do things stand?" Ramón wanted to know, groping for a way to build on whatever the Mexican police already had in place. He'd worked security details for the Houston police many times and knew that local authorities often got so caught up in procedure that they lost momentum and became distracted from the larger picture. For Ramón, getting his brother out of this jam as quickly as possible was all he was focusing on. "This can't go on much longer or someone is really going to get hurt. Seriously hurt. You know?" he reminded Xavier.

"Yeah, yeah. I know," Xavier hurried to acknowledge.

"Where do things stand with Lopez right now?" Ramón asked again.

"I have a stack of fake birth certificates here, at my home, in my safe. I certified them and they're ready for delivery to Lopez. However, the lead investigator down here wants me to stall delivery for another week so the authorities will have more time to put their arrest in motion. I agreed, but I'm nervous as hell about this delay."

"You should be," Ramón stated, certain that Lopez would do anything to get those documents. "If I were you, I'd send Carmen and Linda out of the country," Ramón suggested. "But not to Texas. Maybe to Carmen's parents in Argentina? Could they stay with them until this is settled?"

"Not a good idea," Xavier stated flatly. "Lopez would follow them. My wife and daughter would only be more vulnerable. I'd hate to think of them so far away, with no protection. At least, here in Acapulco, I feel better about the security and can keep an eye on them. No, it's best for all of us to remain here…together… where the police and their undercover people can protect us."

"I hear you," Ramón agreed. "I'm just still in shock over what happened last night. No way was I gonna breach your security system and give those thugs the override codes."

Freshly showered and dressed in a pair of blue shorts and a white T-shirt, Lori lathered lotion over her hands as she hurried down the hallway, following the smell of freshly brewed coffee. However, just before she rounded the corner to enter the kitchen, she paused, surprised by what Ramón was saying. *He wanted Carmen and Linda to go to Argentina to be safe? From what? The thugs who beat him up wanted override codes to breach Xavier's security?* Heart pounding, she bit her lip and listened when Ramón started to speak again.

"Xavier," she heard him say. "I don't feel good about what the authorities in Mexico want you to do. Stalling Lopez is dangerous. Those nasty guys who attacked me won't stop until they get those birth certificates out of your safe, one way or another. They might break into your house while you're in Mexico City. They mean business. You've gotta be careful."

A long pause while Lori tried to piece together what Ramón and Xavier were talking about, knowing that whatever it was, it couldn't be good.

"Don't be a fool," Ramón said. "If they'd slap me around and pull a gun on me, just think what they'd do to Carmen or Linda. Get your family out of Acapulco. Fast."

The force in Ramón's voice sent a chill through Lori, who stepped into the kitchen, a fist propped on her hip.

A shocked Ramón swiveled toward Lori, clearly alarmed by her unexpected intrusion. Lori didn't say a word. She just stood there looking at him in disappointment, her heart pounding, her eyes narrowed in disgust.

Ramón unfastened his gaze from her and focused on the floor, lowering his voice as he told Xavier, "Look man, I gotta go. I'll call you later, okay?"

Lori didn't move, though her eyes tightened into two dark slits. She gazed at Ramón in stone-cold silence, increasing the pressure on him to come clean.

Ramón wiped his jaw with the back of his hand and waited for her to speak. When she didn't, he shrugged both shoulders and lifted his hands, palms toward her. "Okay." He took a backward step. "I guess you overheard?"

"Yeah, I did."

"You heard everything?"

Lori nodded. "Enough."

"Then you must be wondering what this is…all about," Ramón stuttered.

"Damn straight," she snapped.

"I planned to tell you, but I wanted to wait until…"

"Don't try to play me, Ramón," Lori shot back, interrupting him. "I want the truth. Now. What really happened to you last night and how is Xavier involved?"

"All right. I'll tell you, but you've got to promise to keep it to yourself and not interfere."

"Why would I interfere with something that clearly doesn't concern me enough for you to tell me the truth?"

"That's the problem," Ramón hedged, appearing conflicted. "You might be involved and not know it. That's what's worrying me."

Lori swallowed a snappy retort and steeled herself for whatever was coming, determined not to show Ramón how upset she was until she heard him out. Jumping to conclusions would not do any good, but she had to know the truth.

"Sit down," Ramón said, motioning toward the breakfast table, and taking a seat across from her. "Xavier is in trouble."

"I gathered as much," Lori shot back with a fast roll of her eyes.

"Some men in Acapulco are after him to court-certify some fake birth certificates. Probably for illegals to get passports or social security numbers."

"I assume Xavier refused?" Lori pressed. She didn't know Ramón's brother well, but from her short time with him in Acapulco she had gotten the impression that he was an upstanding member of the community and a man who could be trusted to do the right thing.

"Of course he refused, but the local authorities got involved, and asked him to work with them," Ramón replied, proceeding to tell Lori the truth about what had happened in the parking lot the night before. "They ordered me get inside. Told me to give them the override codes that I keep in my safe. I agreed…just to stall them until the police arrived. I was in a tight spot, but luckily, I got away," Ramón said as he explained in detail how everything had gone down.

"So you didn't give up any information?"

"Nope," he concluded.

Lori sat up straighter, eyeing Ramón with concern. "This really sucks, Ramón," she said, lips turned down in disgust. "Security work is more dangerous than I thought."

"Criminals will do anything to get what they want," Ramón replied. "I've never had this happen to me before, but I know of a dealer in Dallas who was kidnapped and held for a week until he gave up the override codes to a wall safe he'd installed in some rich folks' house."

"What happened to him?"

"He was found dead in his car after the heist."

"Damn!"

"Exactly. That's why I'm worried about Carmen, Linda and you, too, of course. If Lopez's men have been watching me, then they're probably watching you."

"Gee, thanks for letting me know that I could be assaulted or possibly killed because of my association with you!" Rising from the table, she moved to the coffeemaker and splashed half a cup of Joe into a mug. Holding her mug, she braced her back against the refrigerator, digesting what he'd told her. "Why didn't you tell me all this last night?"

"I didn't want you to worry."

"That's a hell of a cop-out!"

"No, it's not. I had to talk to Xavier first."

"Why?"

"I just had to, that's all."

"And if you'd told me the truth last night, I doubt we'd have gotten as…as close as we did this morning, huh?"

"Aw, Lori. Don't go there. You gotta know how I feel about you."

"I thought I did, but now I'm not so sure. I trusted you completely, Ramón. I told myself that a man who worked every day to keep people safe would never let me down."

"Trust me, I never will," Ramón protested.

"You already have," Lori countered. She waved a hand back and forth in front of her face, as if clearing the air and clearing her mind. "Listen. I don't want to get any more involved in this little international drama of yours and Xavier's than I am right now. I have enough stress in my life without adding any from you or your family."

"What are you talking about?" Ramón wanted to know.

"That I'm sorry Xavier is in this situation, but there's nothing I can do about it. It's your brother's mess to fix, and if you want to help him, fine. But I can't get involved, okay?"

"Don't overreact," Ramón replied, getting up to walk toward her. "Let's talk this through. You're safe. It's the override codes that Lopez wants, and you don't have access to them."

"You and Xavier can work this out any way you want, but leave me out of it, all right?" Lori stated, steel in her words.

Ramón took a step forward and reached out as if to touch Lori on the shoulder. "I think it might be a good idea if…"

"Stay right there," Lori ordered, her right arm extended to keep him away. No way was she going to let him sweet-talk her out of making her case. Now was not the time for hugs and kisses and words of forgiveness. It was time to get real, get honest and get to the heart of the matter. "Ramón, you deliberately withheld the truth from me. You couldn't even let me in on what you were doing, let alone how serious this is! If this is how you show me you care, then please, stop caring, okay?"

"Don't say that Lori." He took a short step backward, glanced around, grit his teeth and then faced her again, torment in his eyes. "I love you. All I was trying to do was protect you."

"Stop," she said, having heard enough. His stammering confession, and now this sudden need to tell her he loved her? No, that was not what she wanted to hear.

"No, I won't stop," he shot back. "I have to let you know how I feel. I've never fallen in love before, Lori. This is all new to me. Maybe I didn't handle things very well last night, but I was still in shock myself. I promised Xavier that I wouldn't tell anyone about what was going on, so I kept my mouth shut when I shouldn't have."

"Yes, it might have been nice if you'd let me know that you'd decided to gloss over a potentially dangerous situation that might have put my life in danger. What do you think you're doing? Playing supercop or something?"

"That's not funny."

"I don't mean it to be funny," she countered. "This is some serious shit. I guess you didn't tell the police the full truth either, did you?"

"Not completely," he admitted, a slow drag to his words.

"I rest my case."

"The Mexican national police, who're really in charge of the case, are the ones who needed the info. Xavier is going to pass this on to them, and let them coordinate it with the authorities here."

"Maybe you should talk to Clint, Brittany's friend. He might be able to give you some advice."

"I can't do that. I told you," Ramón snapped. "I will not involve the Houston police any more than I already have. I shouldn't have told you anything, but I did."

Lori let loose with a loud cruel laugh, as if she'd heard more than enough. "You know what? I think you'd better go," she decided, surprised when her eyes quickly filled with tears. He'd said he loved her, and she knew she loved him. But how could he love her and put her life in danger? How could she love a man who would lie to her by withholding the truth? How deceitful was that? He'd treated her as if she had no interest in what happened to him, too. Didn't he realize that a huge part of her anger was because *he* was in danger? The thought of anything happening to Ramón made her heart stop and her body go cold. He could have been killed last night. She could be viewing his body in the morgue this morning instead of arguing with him in her kitchen. Didn't he understand how much stress he'd brought into their relationship? Could she handle this? Did she even want to?

"What I was going to say," Ramón continued, breaking into her thoughts. "I think it might be a good idea for me to move in with you. Temporarily. Just until Xavier's situation is resolved and the Mexican authorities have what they need to take Lopez into custody."

"Move in here?" she repeated, certain she had heard him wrong.

"Yes. I don't feel good about leaving you alone."

*He must be confused…suffering aftershocks from the mugging,* Lori calculated, pissed that he'd dare broach the subject of them living together, knowing how upset she was.

"I can take care of myself," she told him in a frigid voice.

"I can do a better job," he countered with great certainty and authority.

"Sorry, I don't think so!" Lori replied, anger suffusing her words. "You knew all along that Xavier was in trouble. You knew it before we ever left Acapulco. When I told you about the strange man lurking on the beach, you dismissed me! That man could have been one of Lopez's thugs…out to harm me. He wasn't a security guard, was he? My God, Ramón, you knew I was exposed back then."

"I'm not sure who that man was, but you're right. He could have been casing the property to see how close he could get. I downplayed my concern because I didn't want to scare you unnecessarily."

Quickly raising her hand, Lori punched Ramón in the chest, and then set down her coffee mug and pummeled him with both fists.

Ramón gripped her hands and held them tightly in his, forcing her to calm down. "I'm really sorry," he apologized.

"You should be!" she yelled, snatching her hands away. When he let her go, she rubbed her wrists and glared at him. "I think it's best if we stay away from each other until this whole mess is settled."

"Don't go overboard."

"I'm not. Give me a call when this is over and then, maybe, we can talk," Lori finished with a snap as her voice cracked in anguish.

"Please, don't say that," Ramón began, pushing back. "Lori. I can handle this. I just need some time to figure out the best way to proceed."

"No, what you need to do is to go. Go home. Go to Acapulco. Go to the police. I don't care…just go away!" Lori shouted, as she yanked open the front door to show him out. "I am so disappointed, I can't talk. Leave. Please. I don't need this kind of drama."

"I'll leave, for now," Ramón calmly agreed. "But you and I are not finished, and I will not let anything happen to you."

"Right," she muttered with skepticism, waving him out the door.

Once he'd left, Lori slumped against the door and burst into tears. Cradling her face in her palms, she shuddered, and then wiped her eyes, determined not to dwell on her misery. *I don't need his sorry ass to keep me safe. I don't want him around. I can take care of myself. I'm better off without him.* But as a fresh round of tears erupted, Lori knew she was fooling herself. The last thing she wanted was to face tomorrow without Ramón in her life.

Angry and sick with disappointment, Ramón got into his truck and drove away from Lori's house. Clearly, he was not going to make any progress with her now, so he might as well go to work and try to get his mind off the mess he'd made of things. He had a big job to complete. He had to pull himself together and focus. Xavier and the trouble he'd caused would have to wait. *But can my relationship with Lori wait, too?* Ramón was worried, terrified of losing her. He was tempted to turn his truck around, go back to Lori and make her understand that he hadn't deliberately meant to hurt her. But what good would that do? he thought. No, he had to stay away. The next time he saw her, the messy situation with Xavier would be settled, and there'd be no more roadblocks to their future. He just hoped she'd be there waiting for him when that happened.

## Chapter 22

Working in the rose garden under a blazing Dallas sun, with her mother at her side, made Lori feel oddly content and she knew why. In the midst of her own emotional turmoil, listening to her mother's chattering complaints about neighbors who neglected their lawns and workers who refused to show up on time allowed Lori to let her troubles slip to the back of her mind.

It was comforting to return to a place that felt familiar, safe and welcoming when her nerves were shot and her dreams destroyed. Tending Trish Myles's perfectly planned, carefully pruned and stately rose garden helped bring order to Lori's chaotic emotions, which fluctuated between anger, disappointment, resentment and regret.

Lori had thought that coming home to Dallas would be exactly what she needed to get a better perspective on her breakup with Ramón. But was it really working? After a week of sleeping in her old bedroom, surrounded by memorabilia of her teenage years, she remained torn and confused. She hated Ramón. She loved him. She missed him like hell, yet never wanted to see him again. She wanted him back, but refused to forgive him for not trusting her. What did she have to do to get him out of her head? He'd dragged her into a dangerous situation, disregarded her right to know what was going on and exposed a selfish side of himself that had really turned her off.

*What else don't I know about him?* she mentally groped, snipping a brittle leaf off a thorny branch with a snap of her pruning shears. What she needed now was time to get him out of her system, breathing space to reset her priorities so she could move forward with no regrets.

"Your birthday's coming up soon," Trish commented, glancing over her shoulder at Lori, who frowned in mock horror at her mother.

"Don't remind me," she mumbled, tugging on the wide straw hat shading her face from the blistering sunlight beaming down on mother and daughter.

"You ought to throw yourself a party," Trish continued, bending to inspect a budding Lincoln Red. "Thirty is a landmark. Have some fun. Get your mind off whatever is making you so grumpy."

Lori paused, pruning shears in midair as she assessed her mother's smug expression. "Grumpy?" Lori repeated, sounding surprised. "I'm not grumpy."

Trish grunted. "You sure aren't acting very happy."

"I'm tired, that's all," Lori defended. "That's why I came to Dallas. To rest."

"Oh, I thought you came to see me," Trish countered, one eyebrow raised.

"You know what I mean," Lori huffed, irritated by her mother's subtle probing.

"No, I don't," Trish replied, tilting her head in concern as she focused on her daughter. "What's wrong, Lori? I know there's something on your mind that you're struggling with. What's got you so down in the dumps?"

A surprising surge of tears welled up in Lori's eyes, making her thankful that her dark sunglasses shielded her eyes from her mother. She didn't want to break down in tears or talk about Ramón or tell her mother how badly he'd disappointed her, so she simply shrugged a noncommittal response, not trusting her voice. "I don't want to talk about it."

"Man trouble?" Trish pressed, clearly not ready to let the conversation end as Lori wanted it to.

"Something like that," Lori relented, realizing that she had to give up some information if she wanted her mother to stop digging for answers. "Things just didn't work out. But don't worry. I'm handling it," she finished.

"Was it Devan? Are you two back together?" Trish prodded, giving Lori a hint of a smile.

"Devan? No! Absolutely not! He's been out of the picture for months," Lori snapped, recalling how much her mother had liked Devan and how difficult it had been for her to convince her mother that they had not been right for each other, without divulging the full story. Her mother never needed to know that Devan had smothered Lori with his love in an obsessive way, or that she'd taken out an order of protection to keep him away. Involving her overly cautious mother in that crazy scenario would have sent Trish Myles over the edge, making everything more difficult than it had been.

"Devan was such a gentleman," Trish crooned. "You two looked so good together. I had high hopes for a wedding. Grandchildren. Marriage brings stability, you know?"

"Drop it, Mom," Lori ordered. "Looks can be deceiving. He might have looked good, but he wasn't who you, or I, thought he was. Anyway, I've gone on with my life. He has, too. Right now, he's doing better than I am, I'd guess."

"Oh? You've heard from him?"

"He sent me a letter. I tore it up. Devan Parker is all in the past."

"Hmm," Trish murmured, squatting down to loosen the soil around a vibrant yellow rose. "Well, if you're not going to have a party for your thirtieth birthday, what do you plan to do?"

Lori sighed, exasperated. "Maybe I'll get drunk on tequila martinis at Enrico's and dance on the tables with strange men. How does that sound?" Lori shot back, flashing a sarcastic grin at her mother and putting an end to their serious conversation.

"Oh, Lori, please. But it wouldn't surprise me if you did do something crazy like that. Nothing you ever do surprises me. You are absolutely fearless."

"That's the best way to live," Lori countered, thinking she might call Brittany and get her to go along with the idea of club-hopping on her birthday. That would be one way to get Ramón Vidal out of her head.

## Chapter 23

As soon as the seat belt light went out, Ramón stood, grabbed his bag from the overhead bin and was first in line to deplane. While waiting for the door to open, he glanced into the forward galley, feeling his heart sink with disappointment that Lori was not standing there, giving him one of her sly, secret smiles to let him know she was as eager as he was to get off the plane and into each other's arms. Suddenly, memories of crowding up against her in the cramped galley space as they zoomed across the sky washed through him, making him blink in surprise that the vision remained so fresh in his mind.

*What's she doing now?* he wondered, trying to visualize her face. Was she watching her phone? Wishing he'd call? Or was she digging in for a long stretch of punishing him because of his stupid miscalculation? *She'll come around. She has to,* he told himself, determined to give her time to cool off, while afraid of losing her altogether.

"Thank you for flying Globus-Americas Airlines," said a well-modulated voice, floating through the cabin, forcing Ramón to look at the woman who was announcing the deplaning instructions. It was Phyllis Marshall, Lori's crew leader, who'd served him during the flight. When Phyllis first greeted Ramón as he boarded, she'd smiled at him in recognition and referred to him by name. Ramón had smiled back, while wondering if she knew that he and Lori had been intimate, that they had shared a wonderful few days together in Acapulco, that they were no longer a couple. Women who worked together talked about that kind of stuff, didn't they? Had Lori been close enough to Phyllis to share such personal information? He hoped not. Moving past Phyllis, he gave her an impersonal nod, stepped into the jetway, and rushed into the terminal.

Walking quickly, Ramón headed down the escalator toward Passenger Pickup, where Xavier would be waiting. As he threaded through the throng of fast-moving travelers, his heart constricted in longing. The last time he'd walked through this airport terminal, Lori had been with him and he had been so happy, unaware that he was about to enter the most sensual and satisfying relationship of his life.

*It was too good to be true,* he thought, saddened by the fact that the dreams he'd had for a life of loving Lori might be gone forever.

A swell of yearning clogged his throat, creating a lump that Ramón didn't like. He'd blown it with Lori. Botched the whole affair, so he'd better stop feeling sorry for himself. If he'd handled things differently, he might be talking to her on the phone right now, making plans to get together when he returned. But she wasn't there, or even speaking to him, and there was nothing he could do about that now.

Swallowing hard, Ramón fought for control of his emotions. He had to focus on what he'd come to Acapulco to do, and then he'd deal with his personal problems.

"Where's Lori?" Xavier asked as soon as Ramón slipped into the Mercedes.

Ramón groaned, letting Xavier know by his mangled response that that was a subject he didn't want to discuss. But knowing there would be no avoiding the subject, he said, "Didn't come in on her flight." Ignoring the look of surprise that Xavier threw at him, Ramón tossed his carry-on bag onto the back seat and settled in to face the windshield, lips pressed into a hard line as if to convey his reluctance to reveal more.

"Oh. I kinda assumed she'd be with you," Xavier commented, ignoring his brother's sullen attitude. "Carmen was looking forward to seeing her again."

Ramón blew air through his lips and sagged back into his seat. "Okay, okay. Here's the deal. We're not together any more."

"What?" Xavier's head swiveled toward Ramón in surprise. "You two were head over heels only a few weeks ago. What's the problem? How'd this happen?"

"Long story, bro," Ramón replied with a shake of his head.

"I've got time."

"Let's just say that my line of work is interfering with our relationship."

"Yeah? How?"

"There are things I have to keep confidential, and apparently that's a problem for her."

"She seemed like a pretty reasonable woman. You telling me everything?"

Ramón simply shrugged.

"So, does your trouble have anything to do with you getting beaten up? She knows what happened to you, and why, right? I know I asked you to keep things quiet, but I assumed you told her over pillow talk…"

Again, Ramón shrugged.

"Stick with her…this will all be over soon," Xavier added.

"Not soon enough for me," Ramón commented.

"Does she know you're in Acapulco now?"

"No. And she can't know anything. I have a plan I want to run past you. If you think it'll work, we've got to give it a try. This may be the only way to solve your problem and get all of us out of this alive."

"I'm game for anything," Xavier replied. "I'm under a hell of a lot of pressure right now and I don't know how much longer I can keep Carmen in the dark about what is really going on. She isn't too happy about the German shepherd guard dog I added to the household. Barks 24/7, but Linda loves him. He sticks to her like glue and won't let strangers get near her."

"Getting a guard dog was a good move," Ramón told Xavier. "But we may have to go in a different direction."

"Let's hear it," Xavier said as he zoomed along the coastal road leading to his house.

"Okay, this is what I think we should do," Ramón began, launching into his plan, anxious for Xavier's reaction. If the authorities agreed to cooperate, they could break Aldo Lopez's fake ID ring without anyone getting hurt. If not, things could become even more dangerous. Ramón knew his plan was risky, but as far as he could tell, it was the only way to go.

# *Chapter 24*

Lori stepped out of the plane and paused at the top of the tall metal stairs to lift her face to the bright Bahamian sunshine. A sweep of tropical warmth bathed her skin with an exotic touch that stirred her sense of independence and adventure. It felt good to be in a beautiful country where balmy nights and white beaches beckoned. An Internet posting she'd come across while surfing travel sites to pass another lonely Saturday night had finally lured her out of her shell of misery. She planned to spend the next three days doing absolutely nothing, especially not thinking about Ramón or the mess he'd made of their relationship. She had another break in her schedule, and it had been a long time since she'd taken a solo pleasure trip like this, and she planned to go dancing, eat whatever she wanted, play tennis and go swimming every day…doing anything and everything possible to get Ramón out of her system and herself back on track.

Lori handed her credit card to the handsome young man working the front desk at the Bahamas Royal Hotel and got lucky.

"How would you like a corner room facing the ocean?" he asked, flashing his blinding white teeth in a generous smile.

"Am I that lucky?" Lori laughed in reply.

"Today, apparently so," he assured her with a grin as he swiped her card and presented her with her room key.

The wraparound veranda of her twenty-fourth-floor luxury suite provided Lori with a spectacular view of the aqua-green water, the huge sailboats in the distance and the sandy-white beach below. Awestruck and giddy with liberation, she looked up into the cloud-free blue sky and laughed. This was exactly what she'd been missing. This feeling of freedom, with its lack of restrictions and accountability, seemed to open her mind so old ghosts could leave. With Ramón out of her life, she'd been adrift, lonely and filled with self-doubt.

Why did the men in her life always disappoint her in the end? Why did she have such bad luck? Just when she was about to give her heart completely to Ramón, he'd yanked her back to reality. *Face it,* Lori, she told herself. *Relationships mean drama, pressure and unnecessary complications. I'm better off keeping it casual and playing the field.*

Within an hour after arriving at the hotel, Lori hit the beach. After a fifteen-minute swim in the cool blue water, she stretched out on a chaise longue under a thatched-palm umbrella with a tall piña colada in her hand. Eyes closed, she luxuriated in the sunshine, allowing every muscle in her body to relax. The sun, the lapping waves and the distant ting-ting of a steel drum band lulled her into a sweet half sleep. Sinking into the tug of dreamland, she dozed under the pleasant sun.

"Another drink, miss?"

Lori jerked alert and stared at the man standing over her. At first, she thought it was Ramón—same build, same longish hair and he even had an earring in his left ear. However, his skin was like delicious milk chocolate and his eyes were shaded by reflective sunglasses that kept her from looking into them.

"What?" she replied, leaning forward.

"Your drink. Looks like the sun has melted all the ice. Would you like me to get you another one?"

Lori glanced at her watered-down drink, looked back up at the man and then smiled. "Sure. Why not?"

"What's your pleasure?" he asked in a voice that sent a tingly pulse through Lori.

"Piña colada," she told him, handing him her glass.

"Be right back. Don't go away," he said, slowly raising his sunglasses to give her a wink.

Lori shook her head, chuckling low in her throat, watching as the stranger took long strides across the sand, heading toward the outdoor bar. He was wearing loose red swim trunks that stopped just above his knees, but his torso was bare, giving Lori a pleasing view of an upper body rippling with muscles that gleamed in the sun. Appreciating what she saw, Lori leaned back and assessed him from the rear, wondering if he was a good dancer...and how he'd react if she asked him to join her in the hotel club tonight. It was time to have some fun, forget about Ramón and lose herself on the dance floor once more.

The band playing in Sunset Harbor, the hotel club off the busy lobby, was one of the best Lori had ever heard. They played a mix of reggae, rock, R&B and jazz that kept the dance floor packed. However, that was just about the only pleasant aspect of her night out with Tyrone, the man she'd met on the beach.

As it turned out, he was a terrible dancer who had difficulty doing anything other than a basic swing step, which he performed in an embarrassing series of erratic moves, reminding Lori of Carlton on *The Fresh Price of Bell-Air*. She had to bite the inside of her cheek to keep from laughing aloud at him, and after two turns on the dance floor, decided to stop the torture.

Now, sitting at their table, she quickly saw that Tyrone preferred to bend his elbow with a drink in one hand and a cigarette in the other than move his feet to the beat of the music. When he ordered his fifth Chivas and Coke, in words that ran together in a frightening slur, Lori excused herself to go to the ladies' room, went straight to the nearest elevator and hurried up to her room.

Kicking off her party shoes, she went out onto the veranda

and stared up at the twinkling stars, a surge of tears swelling in her eyes. She felt disappointed, angry and slightly resentful, as if she'd been slapped in the face.

"What'd you expect from a pickup on the beach?" she reminded herself, knowing what was wrong. She missed Ramón like crazy and wished he'd been with her tonight. But she wanted her safety and independence more. His disregard for her welfare had been inexcusable, making it impossible for her to take him back. She had to move on and forget that he'd broken her heart.

"Oh, Ramón," she moaned, feeling confused about what to do. Obviously picking up strange men in the Bahamas was not the solution. "Ramón will I ever get over you?" she wondered aloud, wiping stray tears from her cheek.

## Chapter 25

As soon as Ramón returned to Houston, he focused like a laser beam on Lori, desperate to patch things up between them. Five days in Acapulco had been the best medicine he could have taken to prepare himself for what he knew he had to do. Sharing his feelings for Lori with Xavier had convinced Ramón that he would not allow what they had to simply slip away. He was going to pursue her until she forgave him. He'd stick like glue to the edges of her life until she took him back. He missed her too much to think he'd ever get over losing her, so that was not an option.

He'd been stupid to keep her in the dark, unprotected and vulnerable to Lopez's men. But that was about to change. Even if she never forgave him, he was going to shift into full protective mode, remaining vigilant until the men involved in the illegal smuggling ring were in custody and the sting operation was over. Besides, tomorrow was Lori's birthday, and the plans they'd made to celebrate on the River Walk in San Antonio were still in place. Maybe he had a chance.

Anxious to hear her voice and reassure himself that he might get through to her, he drove straight to her house and stopped at the curb. Her car was in the driveway. She must be at home. With a jab on his cell phone, he punched in her number, praying she would talk to him.

She did. But her greeting was strained, her voice flat, and in a few mumbled words she let Ramón know that she hadn't budged in her position: she wanted no part of his international drama and wished he'd leave her alone.

"No, I am not going to go to San Antonio with you. And no, I can't see you tonight," Lori shot back.

"But we need to talk," he pressed.

"No, we need to let it go," Lori replied, crushing his hopes for a second chance.

"I'm right outside. I want to come in."

"Don't you dare get out of your car. If you ring my bell, I won't answer the door," she countered, sounding totally serious.

"You can't stop me from telling you that I love you. That I miss you. I don't plan to go away, Lori. I'm going to sit out here until you agree to let me in. I'll stay here all night if I have to."

"That's your choice," she tossed out before disconnecting the call.

Ramón flinched, stung by her recalcitrant attitude. He would never believe that she didn't love him, and he'd never accept her rejection. Settling lower into his seat behind the steering wheel, he turned his face toward her front door, watching Lori's house as the sun began to sink behind her rooftop, almost taking his hopes for a reconciliation with it.

Lori peered out the window and frowned. Dammit, why didn't Ramón just go away? Why couldn't he get it through his head that she wanted nothing to do with him? *Was this a repeat of the Devan Parker experience?* she worried. Surely, Ramón wouldn't force her to take legal action to keep him away, would he? Distraught, she stepped back from the window and went into her kitchen, determined to go about her business as if he were not sitting out there watching her house.

When her phone rang again, she snatched it off the kitchen counter, prepared to tell Ramón to leave or she was going to call the police. However, it was Brittany, who'd just returned from her evening patrol of the subdivision, bringing news that Lori already knew.

"I see Ramón is back," she told Lori, sounding very smug.

"Not in my life, just in my driveway," Lori replied.

"Hmm, he certainly is a determined man," Brittany observed.

"Determined to irritate me," Lori flipped back.

"Maybe you should cut him some slack," Brittany advised. "He didn't actually lie to you."

"As I told you...he lied when he kept his mouth shut. Same thing as far as I'm concerned."

"But maybe he made the right call...keeping you in the dark," Brittany ventured. "After all, he's the security expert. He honors people's privacy for a living. Holding on to confidential information is what he does. I talked to Clint about what happened."

"I told you not to tell anyone!"

"Hey, he's the police. He's cool."

"Whatever," Lori grumbled, now wondering if telling Brittany about Xavier and Ramón's situation had been a good idea.

"Clint sides with Ramón," Brittany went on. "He understands why your man was afraid to let you in on what's going on in Mexico. Giving you too much information could have placed you in danger."

"But now I know everything, so I'm probably even more of a target. Who knows what could happen to me?" Lori fretted.

"Oh, I wouldn't worry. I doubt you're in the mix at all, girlfriend. They tried to strong-arm Ramón and got nothing, so they're long gone back to Mexico. Clint said he doubts there's much of a Houston connection to this thing. The Mexican national police are on top of it. Don't get confused, or overly worried. This isn't a movie and Ramón is no James Bond."

"No, he's not," Lori agreed. "He's a selfish prick who has no idea what he's gotten himself into or what he's done to me."

"Ouch! That's pretty hard."

"Brittany, you know me. I was not looking for a relationship when I met Ramón. All I wanted was a good friend, a good time, but somehow I let it get out of control. See what happened?"

"Well, I'd forgive him if I were you."

"Easy for you to say."

"Anyway… On to another subject. I called to see if we're still on for a night out on the town to celebrate your big Three-O tomorrow."

"Oh. Right," Lori murmured, realizing she'd completely forgotten that she and Brittany had planned a girls' night out to celebrate her thirtieth birthday. It had been a long time since they'd hit the club scene together. With Ramón taking up Lori's social schedule and Brittany's new romance with Detective Washington, they'd drifted away from hanging out together.

"Sure that's okay with Clint?" Lori teased, aware that her friend now spent most of her free time with the handsome detective who partnered with her as they patrolled the subdivision.

"Please," Brittany shot back. "He knows better than to tell me how or with whom to spend my time. I certainly don't tell him. Dating a detective has plenty of drawbacks, and one of them is that his time is not his own. As soon as we decide to go to a movie or out to dinner, he gets called to some domestic violence craziness on the other side of town. We've morphed into real homebodies. Barbecue on the grill and Netflix have become our most trusted social outlets."

"You need to stop," Lori chuckled, knowing Brittany was not complaining. She could tell that her friend was thrilled to have a man like Clint to snuggle up with on her sofa, watching TV. After a tumultuous life in the spotlight, where every bad choice Brittany made and each word she uttered wound up splashed all over the tabloids, Brittany was content to stick around the house and make dinner for her man. She'd finally found peace in an ordinary life in a quiet Houston suburb with a hardworking man who couldn't care less about her past.

"All right then, we're definitely on for tomorrow," Lori confirmed. "Nine o'clock, okay?"

"Fine. Come over when you're ready. I'll be the designated driver," Brittany volunteered. "I've mapped out our evening. First stop—Kinky's. Dirty martinis and their fabulous hot wings.

Next, we move on to Luxe Lounge. Big Dog DJ is gonna be there, so things oughta be lively. Then, I thought we'd swing by Haute Avenue where we can really let our hair down. I love the way that place is lit up. You're gonna have a fabulous time turning thirty."

"I hope so," Lori replied, determined to feel excited about spending her birthday club-hopping with her friend instead of with Ramón, in a hotel suite in San Antonio's most romantic district, wrapped in his arms and cocooned in their love.

# Chapter 26

The next evening, when Lori stepped onto Brittany's front porch and rang the doorbell, she was in a much better mood than the day before. She was wearing her favorite red silk sheath and gladiator spike heels with gold buckles, and she'd spent the morning at the salon getting her hair and nails done to perfection. Her upswept do and flawless makeup made Lori feel sexy, energized and ready for an evening of nothing but fun.

It took longer than usual for Brittany to answer her doorbell, and when she did, Lori was surprised to see that her friend was wearing a white terry bathrobe and was not yet dressed. "Running late?" Lori remarked as she entered Brittany's foyer and walked over to a spouting-lion fountain in the art niche.

"Yeah," Brittany confirmed with a grin of regret as she tightened the belt of her robe. "Go on into the living room. There's some champagne on ice, cork popped. Get started while I get dressed."

"Why not?" Lori agreed, moving into the luxuriously appointed den where soft tan couches and deep club chairs held too many throw pillows to count. The scent of cinnamon and lilac filled the air, along with soft music coming from Brittany's iPod on the glass-topped coffee table. Lori went over to the bar, reached for the bottle of champagne, and then gasped when she saw her mother walk out of Brittany's kitchen carrying a tall white cake covered in pink roses and lit with a blaze of candles.

"Surprise!" Trish Myles called out to her daughter, grinning with delight.

"What's going on?" Lori shouted, as the room suddenly filled with people. Secret partiers emerged from the back of the house, down the spiral staircase, revealing themselves from their hiding places. Four of Lori and Brittany's sorority sisters popped into the room wearing crazy party hats. Janice and Tom Evans, the young couple who'd recently moved into the neighborhood, entered and began to toss out colorful party streamers. Everyone began hugging Lori and screaming, "Happy Birthday," clearly thrilled that they had blindsided her.

Shocked by the overwhelming crowd as well as the surprise flood of affection, Lori's eyes began to water. "How in the world did you…?" she stammered, barely able to speak. "This is…oh my God!" Lori shouted when her flight crew members—Phyllis, Sam and Allen—stepped through the front door, grinning from ear to ear.

"Where'd you all come from?" she gasped. "I didn't see any cars in the driveway."

"I arranged for valet parking down the street," a deep voice from behind informed her.

Lori whirled around and faced Clint Washington, obviously one of Brittany's cohorts in planning this stunning surprise. Lori went over to Clint and gave him a hug. "You're in on this, too?"

"That's right. The community-watch program out here is working so well, I've got too much extra time on my hands."

"Don't believe him!" Brittany quipped, coming up beside Clint.

"Brittany, this is all too much," Lori protested with a shake of her head.

"Not for my best friend!" Brittany shot back as she slipped

out of her terrycloth robe to reveal a gorgeous green designer wrap dress underneath. "This is exactly the kind of celebration you deserve."

"You knew all along we weren't going clubbing, didn't you?" Lori gasped, faking irritation.

"Sure did," Brittany replied, matching Lori's frown with a smug expression. "But I have to give credit to your mom. She called me, gave me the idea and really helped pull this together."

As if on cue, Trish moved deeper into the room, still holding the blazing cake. "You really didn't think I'd let you turn thirty without a party, did you?" Trish challenged with a hint of a smile.

"Or get by with only going clubbing with me, did you?" Brittany added as she guided Lori toward the towering cake that Trish placed on the dining room table. "Make a wish! Blow out the candles! Let's get this party started."

Feeling totally overwhelmed and thrilled with all the celebratory fuss, Lori did as instructed, pausing to close her eyes to make a silent wish. *I wish for emotional peace,* she thought, not about to ask for anything more specific. With Ramón's disappointing behavior still rattling her cage, all she wanted was freedom from worry about whether or not she'd done the right thing breaking off with him. After sucking in a deep breath, Lori leaned down and blew out every candle in one try, making everyone laugh and clap their hands.

"You'll get the first piece," Trish told her daughter, admiring the frothy confection.

"Hold it for me," Lori replied, wanting to take her time getting into the mix.

"Before you all dive into the cake, we've got food and music, too," Brittany announced, escorting Lori across her den to throw open the French doors leading to her patio. Lori shrieked in delight when she saw Big Dog DJ standing behind his keyboard, ready to get the music going, and a long buffet table covered in food.

With a salute to Lori, the husky music man pressed a button and sent the silky voice of Kanye West into the room, starting the fun. Immediately, everyone began eating, talking, laughing and diving into the lavish buffet that Brittany had spread out on tables around the pool. Lori was first in line to sample the shrimp scampi, her favorite seafood dish.

"Enjoy your getaway in the Bahamas?" Phyllis inquired as she stepped up to the table next to Lori.

"Oh, yeah," Lori replied, glancing at her coworker. "It was fabulous. Only wish I could have stayed a few days longer."

"Why the Bahamas? I was surprised you didn't go to Acapulco when Ramón returned to Mexico."

"Oh?" Lori commented with a lift of a brow. "He went to Acapulco?"

"Yeah, he was on my flight last week." A beat. "And before you ask, no, I didn't talk to him other than to serve him just like any other passenger."

"I wasn't going to ask," Lori replied with a slight snip. "He can come and go as he pleases. We don't keep tabs on each other."

"Oh, it's like that, huh?"

"Yeah, it's like that."

"Well," Phyllis stated. "Speaking about getaways. I have five days' vacation coming up. Been thinking of going to Seattle to visit my sister. Would you be able to fill in as flight leader for me while I'm gone?"

"Sure, if you clear it with the boss," Lori agreed, grateful for the vote of confidence. Flight leader positions were hard to come by and this might be just the opportunity she needed to show her boss that she was ready to move up.

"No problem," Phyllis added. "I ran it past him yesterday. You're already approved."

"Great! So when are you leaving?" Lori asked.

"I'm shooting for next Thursday, return the following Monday. As soon as I get my travel plans in place, I'll let you know."

"Okay, I'll keep the days open." Lori added a crispy crab puff to her plate as she continued talking. "You do need a vacation, Phyllis. I can't remember when you've taken a day off."

"Me, either," Phyllis laughed, moving further along the table to pile more goodies on her plate. "I'll be calling…"

"I'll be ready," Lori called back as more guests came over to congratulate her.

The party was such a pleasant surprise. Lori couldn't help but think about how lucky she was. She had good friends who cared about her. Coworkers who trusted and respected her. A mother who had gone to great lengths to make sure Lori had a genuine surprise party.

*Isn't this what emotional peace is all about?* she thought, knowing her wish had already been granted.

"So, Lori, how's your friend, Ramón, doing these days?" Clint inquired as he reached past Lori to spear a piece of grilled chicken.

"All right...I guess," Lori replied, as if the name meant little to her. First Phyllis, and now Clint. Why was everyone so damn concerned about her relationship with Ramón? "Haven't seen him for a while, but he was doing fine the last time I saw him."

"I've kept my eye on his assault case, but there hasn't been any progress on apprehending the men who roughed him up."

"Too bad," Lori murmured, doubting Ramón had given the police enough information to make a concerted effort at catching them.

"Somebody you know was attacked?" Tom Evans remarked, entering the conversation, his petite wife at his side.

Lori squinted at Clint, warning him to keep mum. "A friend," Lori told Tom. "But he wasn't hurt too badly, that's the good part."

"Random attack?" Tom probed as he sipped his margarita.

"Think so," Lori hedged.

"Those kinds of attacks are much too common nowadays," Tom added.

"Tell me about it," Lori agreed with a fast blink of her eyes.

"At least our community-watch program is helping a lot," Janice Evans added, focusing on Clint. "Thanks to you, Detective Washington."

"And Brittany, too," he added.

Janice nodded in agreement. "I see you two driving around the neighborhood all the time. You've really made Brightwood a safer place to live and we appreciate your efforts."

Accepting Janice's praise, Clint nodded. "I have to admit there haven't been any more vandalism incidents in Brightwood since we started the community watch patrols, so something must be working."

"That's very reassuring for homeowners like us," Tom commented, glancing at his wife. "We just installed a Vida-Shield deluxe security system. That, along with the community-watch program, gives us a lot of peace of mind."

"That's good," Lori stated, thinking back to the day Ramón had installed her system, when she was totally wrapped in his love. She finished off her crab puff and set her empty plate on a nearby table. "Gotta go mingle. You keep up the good work," she told Clint with a nod, stepping out of the conversation.

"Lori! Come over here," Trish called her daughter's name while waving a hand.

Lori pivoted around and watched as her mother crossed the patio in hurried steps.

"You'll never guess who's here," Trish said in a rush of words, sounding excited.

"Who?" Lori asked, scanning the area.

"There!" Trish replied, pointing to a man who was emerging from the house.

Lori gasped in shock. Mouth open, she shot a hard zinger at her mother and then looked straight into her surprise guest's eyes, her stomach lurching as she realized he looked even more handsome than the last time she'd seen him.

"Devan!" The name shot out of Lori's mouth like a dart thrown at a board.

"Yeah, it's Devan," Trish confirmed, looking very pleased with herself. "I invited him as my special guest," she confessed. "Doesn't he look great?"

*Yes, he damn sure does,* Lori thought, a tingle of excitement, tinged with apprehension, running through her body.

"Hello, Lori." Devan moved from behind Trish, stopped in front of Lori and locked eyes with her. "I hope you're not angry that I came."

"He didn't crash the party," Trish reminded her daughter.

"That's right. Your mother called me, insisted I drop by. I

promise not to stay long, but I did want to see you...and wish you a happy birthday."

Still speechless, Lori gave Devan a tepid smile and then glared at her mother, afraid to say what was really on the tip of her tongue. *This certainly isn't going to contribute to my emotional calmness,* she thought, forcing a smile of greeting.

"Hi. This *is* a surprise," she said, struggling to keep her voice from cracking, while Trish Myles shrugged her shoulders, lifted one hand in surrender, and gave her daughter a sheepish grin.

"Don't be mad," Trish defended. "After you told me about Devan's letter, and how much he wanted to stay in contact, I decided to call him. We chatted, and then I thought, why not let Lori see for herself how he's doing? And here he is."

"That's right, Lori. I owe you so much. As I said in my letter..."

"You're welcome to stay," Lori interrupted, desperate to keep her mother out of her and Devan's business. What else could she say? She couldn't offend him or say anything that sounded stupid. Just when she'd begun to get a handle on her emotions, her mother had to pull this crazy stunt?

Seeing Devan again was not easy. Old feelings rushed back and crowded her heart. Today, his sharp ebony features defined a face that seemed calmer, more mature and more open than she remembered. His immaculate attire, coupled with his new, more humble demeanor struck a chord deep inside Lori that began to melt her resolve.

How could she be mad at him when he'd taken the time to write her a letter, to thank her for helping him recover from a difficult period in his life? How could she blast her mother for inviting him to the party after all the work she'd done to pull this celebration off? No, now was not the time to say or do something she might regret, and ruin the party for everyone. She'd hold it together, ride out this turbulent patch and believe that calmer seas were just ahead.

"Can we talk for a minute?" he asked, giving her that same crooked half smile that had hooked her in the elevator of the parking garage the first time they met.

"Uh, Mom, excuse us?" Lori prompted, gracing her mother

with a withering look that sent Trish hurrying back inside the house. "Let's sit over there," Lori suggested, gesturing toward a table away from the music and the food.

Why not listen to what Devan had to say? He'd told her he wasn't going to stick around very long, and this unexpected encounter might be just what she needed to close the book on the odd mix of feelings she had about the way their relationship had ended.

Once they were seated, Devan took the lead in describing his therapy sessions and what he had learned about himself, apologizing for all the trouble he had caused.

"I'm not a lifesaver," she told Devan. "I did what I thought was best…for both of us." Lori spoke in as cool a tone as she could manage.

"I know this is difficult," Devan started. "I shouldn't have come, huh?"

"No. It's okay. Really. I'm not angry about you being here. In fact, I'm glad to know you're doing so well," she replied, adopting a calm, respectful tone.

"I see things so much differently now," he admitted to Lori. "Therapy opened my eyes. I was so off base with you. I didn't know how to maintain a realistic relationship with a woman, and I was very selfish."

"That's all in the past," Lori commented, reaching out to touch the back of his hand. "I think we all have issues that we have to work through. At least you've cleared up some baggage, and can go on."

"I shouldn't have been so frightened about losing you."

"But I wasn't going to leave. You pushed me away by smothering me."

"I know, and I was wrong. Lori…"

"Hey, birthday girl," Brittany interrupted, stopping to look down at Lori and Devan, clearly curious about what was going on. "Excuse me. Hate to break in on your conversation, but another guest just arrived," she announced. "Someone I thought you might want to greet personally," she prompted with a cut of her eyes and a tilt of her head toward the far side of the pool.

Lori followed Brittany's gesture and swept her gaze across

the blue-green water to fasten her eyes on Ramón, standing with his arms folded on his chest, looking directly at her.

Lori scowled at Brittany, curled her bottom lip, and then said, "Oh, no, you didn't."

"Oh, yes, I did," Brittany admitted, turning her attention to Devan. "I wanted *all* of Lori's friends to be here to wish her a happy birthday. Hope you don't mind if I steal her away for a quick minute."

"Uh, not at all," Devan stuttered, clearly confused. "I was leaving anyway." He turned to look at Lori. "Can I call you?"

A moment passed while Lori considered his request, reeling from the fact that Ramón had started walking her way. "Sure. Call me. We'll finish our conversation, okay?"

"I'll hold you to that," Devan told her, rising from the table and walking away.

"Brittany!" Lori muttered under her breath as soon as Devan was out of earshot. "What were you thinking? This is all too much! You *and* my mom need to stay out of my business."

"Too late," she tossed back just as Ramón arrived and forced Lori to look up at him, confusion in her eyes.

"Brittany asked me to drop by. All right?" Ramón probed, clearly testing Lori's reaction.

"Well, I guess it has to be," Lori shot back, glancing from Ramón to Brittany, before letting out an exasperated sigh. When Ramón sat down in the seat that Devan had just vacated, Lori remained silent, as if expecting Ramón to give her some clue as to why she should talk to him.

"You know, I think I'm gonna get some more champagne," Brittany decided, easing away from the couple.

"So, do you have any news?" Lori prompted when the silence dragged on, certain he must have come to tell her that the people involved in the illegal immigration ring were behind bars and Xavier was out of danger.

"Unfortunately, no," Ramón replied, sitting back in his chair, blowing air through his lips. "But I couldn't stay away any longer. I'm lost without you, Lori. These past few weeks have been pure hell. I love you. I refuse to let this separation drag on any longer! Come back to me. Please. We can get through this together."

"Xavier and his family are still in danger?" Lori asked, lower lip pouted out.

"Yes," Ramón admitted, his voice tense with frustration.

"Then we have nothing to talk about," Lori snapped in sharpened words. He knew the conditions she'd set on resuming their relationship and she wasn't going to budge.

Ramón hunched forward, fingers knotted into his palms, as if determined to make her listen. "In a few more days, this'll all be over."

Lori frowned, not even wanting to get into that conversation. What she wanted was peace of mind, a chance to enjoy her party and another drink. "Ramón, would you get me another glass of champagne?" she requested, deciding she needed some fortification to get through this. First, Devan. Now, Ramón. How did her plans for a fun-filled evening of nightclubbing with Brittany turn into this nightmare of stress?

"Sure. Champagne coming right up. Stay put. I have a lot more to say to you, okay?" Ramón said, scraping back his chair on the cement patio as he stood and strode away.

Not two seconds after Ramón had left, Devan reappeared, leaned down and placed his hand beneath Lori's chin as he whispered in her ear. "I'm leaving, but I have to ask one question before I go."

*Damn,* she thought he was long gone. What was it going to take to shake this guy? "What?" Lori asked, tensing under his touch.

"Have dinner with me," Devan murmured in her ear, his lips barely brushing her cheek.

"I don't think…"

"Just dinner that's all. I want to show you how different it can be with us. I think the world of you. Let me prove to you that I'm not the man I used to be."

Why did he have to do this? Complicating everything and pushing his luck? She struggled with her answer, knowing his plea sounded sincere. Deep in her heart, she knew he loved her. Perhaps too much. And that was probably what had driven him to such extremes. But at least he'd been honest about his feelings. He had never lied to her. He'd never put her in any real danger. Dropping her defenses, Lori impulsively nodded. "Okay. Dinner."

"Tomorrow? I can pick you up around eight," Devan pressed.

Catching a glimpse of Ramón walking toward her, holding two glasses of champagne, she raised her voice. "Yes, dinner tomorrow will work fine," she told Devan, wanting to give Ramón something to think about. Lori stood, leaned toward Devan and kissed him quickly on the lips. "It *was* good to see you, Devan. Thanks for coming. See you tomorrow."

"Thank your mother," Devan replied in the sexy tone that Lori remembered too well. "I'm outta here."

"At eight?" Lori repeated, knowing Ramón had overheard everything. She hoped he was as devastated as she was that their love affair had hit a rough patch and stalled in midair, ruining the journey she had longed to take with him.

Ramón watched, infuriated that Lori would play him like this. Who was that guy and how long had she known him? Obviously, long enough to kiss him in public as if she really cared. Ramón's jealousy flared and his stomach tightened. He didn't want to lose Lori, but what right did he have to interfere? With a crack, Ramón placed the two glasses of champagne on a nearby table, turned around and left. He knew exactly what he had to do to prove his love for Lori, and once she was back in his arms, he'd never let her go.

# Chapter 27

*Heavenly. Fantastic. Sublime.* Those were the words that flitted through Lori's mind as she sat across from Devan and sipped the most delicious cabernet sauvignon she had ever tasted. From their secluded table on the tropically landscaped veranda of the Sugar Hill Country Club, she assessed her surroundings and sighed in satisfaction. Music drifted from inside, where a hip, edgy jazz combo called the Uptown Five performed a catchy rendition of "Living for the City" by Stevie Wonder, one of Lori's favorite songs. Unable to keep still, she started humming along with the saxophone, tapping her fingers on the white tablecloth and swaying gently from side to side.

"Great group," she commented, smiling at Devan, who nodded his agreement. "It's been a long time since I've heard anyone do Stevie so well."

"I thought you'd enjoy this group," he commented. "Remember that Stevie concert we went to in Austin?"

"Yeah, it was raining like crazy and we were soaking wet by the time we finally got inside the arena."

"But it didn't take long for us to dry out, with all the dancing in the aisles we did."

Lori tilted back her head and chuckled low in her throat, allowing memories of her good times with Devan to surface. "Oh, yeah. That was one night I won't forget."

Devan hunched over his glass of wine and reached out to touch Lori on the cheek, allowing his finger to rest near her temple as he spoke. "I've never forgotten any moment, day or night, that we spent together," he told her in a whispery voice that brought Lori's eyes to his. "I mean it, Lori. If I had to, I'll bet I could give you details of every date we had. Every kiss you ever gave me and every laugh we shared."

Lori swallowed in surprise, both flattered and uneasy. Devan's love for her had not wavered at all. He remained as steadfast in his feelings as he'd been when they were together. But was that normal or unusual? She wasn't sure what such devotion meant, but one thing she did know: he had changed, and she wasn't going to overanalyze the situation.

This was her third date with Devan since hooking up with him at her birthday party two weeks before, and he hadn't pressured her at all. What they shared were chaste goodnight kisses at her front door. No hands all over her body, and no requests to come inside her house. In fact, he was giving her so much space she was beginning to wonder about him. He certainly *had* changed!

Going out with Devan *was* helping her get over Ramón, who had simply vanished. Ramón Vidal was out of the picture and Devan was back in. She had to look to the future, not to the past, just as Devan was doing. Spending time with him was helping her move on.

Tipping back her wineglass, Lori finished her drink and then checked her watch. It was close to twelve-thirty. Definitely time to call it a night. She lifted an eyebrow in question at Devan, who caught her meaning immediately.

"One last dance before we go?" he asked, already pushing back his chair to stand.

"Of course. We can't let this wonderful music go to waste," Lori replied, taking Devan's arm as they walked across the veranda and stepped onto the dance floor.

Snuggling against Devan's broad chest, she felt relaxed and safe. Was it the wine? The music? Or had she finally found the emotional calm she'd been searching for for so long? Her time with Ramón had been a chaotic mix of good times, adventure, and great sex—impulsive behavior that had fulfilled her wish for a no-strings-attached liaison. Ramón had brought an edgy kind of risk taking into her life that had blinded her to the reality of just how dangerous a relationship with him would be. Maybe this slower pace that Devan was offering was what she needed right now.

When the music stopped, Lori left the country club. After arriving at her house, Devan pulled into the driveway and reached out to take Lori's hand.

Lori sank back in her seat and closed her eyes, while soft music filled the car.

"I had a great time," Devan told her, running his thumb across the back of her hand.

"Hmm, me too," Lori murmured, turning to face Devan and accept the kiss he placed on her lips.

"Things are good between us, aren't they?" he gently probed, brushing his fingertip across Lori's cheek.

Lori simply smiled and blinked, acknowledging his inquiry.

"Better than before?" he went on, edging closer, reaching out to pull her near.

"I think so," she agreed with a shift to move closer, allowing the magic of their night to take over.

"Good enough to move what we've got to the next level?" he ventured, whispering his request as he traced a finger along her bare arm.

Tensing, Lori pulled away and captured Devan's eyes, feeling uneasy with his request. Sex with Devan was not on her agenda, and she prayed he wasn't going to push too hard and ruin everything. "You mean...you want to come in?" she said with hesitation, easing out of his embrace.

"No, I mean...I want you to marry me," Devan stated, sounding completely serious.

"Oh, Devan, don't go there. Not again."

"Why not?"

"It's too soon."

"How can it be too soon? You know me. And you know I've loved you for a long time, Lori. Now that I have my problems under control and we're back on track, why should we wait?"

Lori slid to the far side of the passenger seat and pressed her back against the window. "I don't want to marry you, Devan."

"Why? Is it because of that other guy you've been dating?"

Lori flinched, chin raised in surprise. "No. I don't want to marry anyone, and how do you know who I've been dating, anyway?"

"I just do, that's all. And I can tell you right now, he's not the one for you. He's in some kind of trouble, because he's been to the North Side Police Command Station four times in the past two weeks."

"What?" Lori spat out, stunned at how casually Devan dropped that bomb on her. "How do you know that?" she demanded.

"I just do."

"You've been following Ramón?"

"No, checking him out. And I can tell you, he's no good."

Lori watched Devan's face turn hard and mean, as his voice deepened when he pressed his demands.

"I'm the man for you, Lori," he went on. "You're wasting your time fooling around with a guy who doesn't deserve you. Marry me...I could make you happy."

"Stop it, Devan," Lori ordered, horrified to see the old Devan resurface before her eyes. This was like a replay of a bad movie she'd hoped she would never see again and she was getting out. Reaching for the door handle, she told Devan, "I'm going inside. Don't bother to walk me to the door. In fact, I don't think you should bother to call me again. Apparently, this isn't going to work after all."

"It could if you'd let it!" Devan shouted, his words rife with anger. "You just need to give me a chance! No man will ever love you the way I do. It's me or no one, Lori. You know that, don't you?"

"Is that a threat?" Lori shouted, challenging his rambling, anger-filled tirade.

"No, just the truth, and you'd better remember it," Devan spat back, his features turning hard and mean.

When he tried to grab hold of Lori's arm, she pushed him away and opened the car door. Stumbling out, she ran across the lawn to her entry, but before inserting her key into the lock, she glanced back. At least he had been smart enough not to follow her.

Once inside, she went into her bedroom and slumped down on her bed, trembling as she tried to wrap her mind about what had just happened.

*How could I have been so stupid to believe he'd changed? What in the world was I thinking?*

She heard a car engine turn over. Cautiously, she went to the window at the front of the house and peered between the slats in the blinds. His car was still there, with the engine running and the headlights off. She gulped in fear, aware that he was sitting behind that dark windshield, watching her, resenting her and fuming mad that she'd turned down his proposal. He'd never used such an angry tone with her before, and his threatening words hung in Lori's mind like grenades primed to explode.

*What is he going to do?* she worried. Launch another bombardment of e-mails and phone calls as he had before? Pressure her until she went to court, again?

*Oh, God I hope not,* Lori silently moaned. The thought of going through that made her stomach contract in knots of fear. Devan was much more unstable than she'd thought, so who knew what he might do to get back at her for rejecting him now? *He's a sick, twisted man who's been spying on me...and Ramón, too!*

Lori pressed a hand to her mouth. *I know he's plotting something, but what?* she fretted, glancing into the dark street, recalling the sinister look on Devan's face when she rejected him the second time. *What is it going to take to make this man leave me alone?* she wondered, blinking back tears she refused to let fall. Between Devan and Ramón, she'd had enough of crying and feeling sad. It was time to toughen up, take control and, perhaps, forget about men altogether.

# Chapter 28

At three in the morning, Ramón lay awake, his thoughts shifting between his anger over the way he'd bungled things with Lori and the fast-approaching resolution to Xavier's precarious situation. He hated to think of Lori dating that guy he'd seen her kiss at the party, but Brittany had confirmed everything, filling him in on who he was, while promising not to tell Lori that they'd talked. Brittany had told Ramón that Devan Parker was an old flame of Lori's whom her mother adored and hoped her daughter would marry.

Ramón gritted his teeth in irritation. Going up against a man who had the approval of a woman's mother was a hard row to hoe, and after seeing the way Lori had flirted with the guy at her party, he could tell that she still had feelings for him.

Ramón gazed into the dark void of his bedroom, trying to figure Lori out. If she truly loved him, she wouldn't have pushed him away so quickly. If she cared about his feelings, she would have spared him the embarrassment of watching her kiss another man!

Ramón groaned and rolled onto his side, missing her so much

it made his stomach churn. This was all his fault. She'd told him from the beginning not to expect too much, too soon. She'd wanted to go slow, making no commitment, but he hadn't been able to keep his emotions in check. God, how he wanted her back. But he would not approach her and try to make things right until he'd done what he had to do for Xavier.

Ramón pulled in a slow, calming breath. *It was almost over.* According to Xavier, the Mexican authorities were poised to make their sweep of arrests at any moment and were working with Immigration and Customs Enforcement (ICE) to identify an American connection in the case. ICE officials had learned that someone working both sides of the Texas/Mexico border was helping Lopez get illegals into the States and they were determined to nab this key person when they busted the ring.

Hopefully, the whole nasty affair wouldn't drag on much longer. But was he willing to risk losing Lori while he waited?

When Lori's outside motion sensor illuminated her driveway, the sudden flood of light jerked her from an unsettling dream, in which she'd been walking down the aisle with Devan. Relieved to realize that the wedding ceremony was not really happening, she rubbed her eyes and focused on the lime-green clock glowing next to her bed. Three-twenty in the morning. All the wine she had drunk at dinner with Devan had left her feeling a bit woosy and unfocused. Sitting up, she cocked her head to the side and listened for any unusual sounds. With the improved security system Ramón had installed, along with Clint's assurance that the neighborhood was safer than ever, she wasn't particularly worried. Her motion-sensor light had come on many times in the middle of the night. A strong wind, a passing car that stopped to turn around in her driveway, even a hard rain could set it off. Even Brittany had caused an alert last week when she crossed Lori's yard to slip a piece of misdirected mail into Lori's mail slot. But it couldn't be Brittany tonight, Lori realized, because her neighbor was in San Francisco pitching her TV sitcom script to an interested producer.

Getting out of bed, Lori went to the window and peeked

between the slats in her plantation shutters. "Oh, it's just a stray cat," she murmured watching as a large yellow tom raced down her driveway and ducked into some shrubs.

Three short beeps, followed by a long whistling sound pulled Ramón out of the sleep he'd finally managed to find. The alert startled him awake, forcing him to concentrate, as it was not the sound of his home or auto security alarm. Sitting up, he remained still, allowing his mind to clear.

"Lori!" he shouted, fear suddenly gripping him. Jumping out of bed he grabbed his cell phone and pressed the button to interrupt the beeping alarm, certain she was in danger.

Though Lori didn't know it, when Ramón installed her new burglar system, he'd also connected his cell phone to her outside motion alarm in order to monitor her property. He hadn't done it to intrude on her privacy or to keep track of her every move, but to make sure the kids who'd vandalized her house would be arrested if they tried it again. The custom-made heat sensor he'd put into her motion-sensitive monitor was designed to alert him if any living thing larger than an average dog got within two feet of her bedroom window after dark.

At the time he added the feature, he'd had no idea that it would be needed to protect her from Lopez's men as well.

Now, someone was either lurking around Lori's house or trying to get in. Ramón had to get over there and find out what was going on.

He slid into his jeans, pulled on shoes and a shirt, snatched his keys off his dresser and got into his car, knowing that her system would simultaneously summon the police. But who knew how long it would take them to respond?

Driving as fast as he could and still be safe, Ramón arrived at Lori's house before the police, zooming into her driveway as his headlights illuminated the front lawn, the garage and the length of the drive, where he saw the outline of a person crouching low among the shrubs.

"Hey!" Ramón shouted, jumping out of his truck. He reached into the bed of his truck and grabbed a heavy pipe wrench from his toolbox, prepared to fight, if he had to. When the figure did not move, Ramón boldly crept closer, his weapon raised, his heartbeat racing from the surge of adrenaline that pumped through his body. When the shadowy figure stirred, Ramón lunged forward, swinging the pipe wrench outward, striking the man across the back. "Get up! Get outta there!" he ordered, firming his stance over the intruder, weapon high in the air. "The police are on their way, Buster, so don't you dare try anything. If you do, you'll be sorry."

However, Ramón's warning fell on deaf ears. In a flash of black, the crouching figure rose, hit Ramón with a hard shove that sent him facedown on the cement, and took off.

"Hell, no!" Ramón yelled, recovering quickly. Without a nanosecond of hesitation he sped off after the man, illuminated by the yellow swath of light beaming from Ramón's truck headlights. Ramón flinched to see the flash of a blade from the knife the man was holding, while his dark ski mask and gloves added to his sinister appearance. When the blurry shadow hit the street, Ramón increased his pace. He chased the figure across Lori's neighbor's lawn and tackled him at the curb, sending both of them rolling into the middle of street. With a grunt, Ramón grabbed the man by the shoulders, flipped him onto his back, straddled him and jammed his pipe wrench across the intruder's throat. As he pressed his weapon against the man's neck with one hand, he used the other to rip off the ski mask, which he flung into the air.

"Damn!" Ramón cursed, when he realized who it was. "It's you! You asshole! What the hell do you think you're doing?" he shouted just as Lori burst out of her front door and raced into the street.

"What's happening?" Lori screamed at Ramón, clutching her bathrobe over her nightgown. "What's going on?"

"See for yourself," Ramón told her, waving his pipe wrench in front of the angry man, who glared back at him with murder in his eyes.

Lori let out a scream. "Oh, my God. Devan! What are you doing here?" Lori yelled, a fist pressed to her lips.

"Looks like your boyfriend is a Peeping Tom...or worse," Ramón managed, while taking in huge gulps of air.

"I can't believe this," Lori started. "Ramón! Where did you come from? How did you know...?"

"I promised to keep you safe, didn't I?" Ramón interrupted.

Lori didn't respond, but simply fastened a serious stare on Ramón and sank down beside him on her knees.

Ramón felt his entire body go on alert. His heart was racing like crazy. His mouth felt as if he'd swallowed a bucket of sand. And his lip, which he could tell was bleeding again, pulsed with spikes of pain. But he didn't care. All he cared about was winning Lori's respect and trust, because after tonight, there was no way he'd ever leave her again.

# Chapter 29

Ramón returned to Lori's house after accompanying the police when they took Devan in. It was daybreak now, and after the exhausting ordeal of giving his statement to the authorities, he was wide awake, hyped up and hungry.

"Devan actually confessed to vandalizing my house?" Lori remarked when Ramón finished telling her about his chat with the police.

"Sure did," Ramón replied, sitting down at the kitchen table, which Lori had set for breakfast. "He was acting like a crazy man. Kept screaming something about teaching you a lesson. That you weren't as smart as you thought you were and how easily he'd fooled you into thinking he'd changed."

"Damn," Lori muttered, stunned by the realization that Devan had been watching her all along, toying with her emotions and setting her up for a disastrous end. How ironic that Devan had been the one to bring danger into her life, and not Ramón, as she'd thought.

Lori placed a plate of eggs, ham and toast in front of Ramón, poured him a second cup of coffee and then sat down across from him, cupping her own coffee mug between her palms.

"I hope Devan rots in jail!" she stated, seething with anger. He'd terrorized her, violated her home, eroded her sense of safety. Because of what he'd done to her house, the residents of Brightwood had initiated a community-watch program, thinking they were under attack by a bunch of teenage vandals. "What a loser," Lori said with a sigh of deflation, filled with disgust for Devan.

"Yeah," Ramón responded between bites of toast. "The cops booked him on charges of vandalism, trespassing and intent to do bodily harm because he was carrying that knife, which he obviously planned to use on you. He could have done some serious damage, but now he's going to do some serious time."

"He'd better," Lori replied, shocked that Devan had been so unbalanced. She mentally kicked herself for actually believing he had changed and gotten help.

"So what's the real story on you and him?" Ramón asked, setting down his fork to level a questioning look on Lori. "Don't you think I deserve to know?"

"Yes, you do," Lori agreed with a lift of her chin, as if gathering the courage to explain. In halting words she told Ramón about her relationship with Devan—how they'd met and how quickly they'd become intimately involved, leading to Devan's expectations of marriage. "After I finally got Devan out of my life and into counseling, I promised myself that I would never get seriously involved with a man unless I'd known him for a long, long time. No more surprises, you know?" she finished, hoping Ramón now understood why she'd shied away from getting too serious with him.

When Ramón nodded in understanding, she continued. "Devan had been acting so normal lately, that I believed his therapy had worked, that he was not so possessive anymore. Boy, was I wrong. He really had me fooled. Everything about him was a sham." She paused, expecting Ramón to make some snide comment about her poor judgment, but when he didn't, she leaned back in her chair, grateful for his silence. "And everyone thought some neighborhood kids had spray painted my house. It was Devan all along. Sicko."

"Exactly. Proves my point. You can never really know what a person is capable of doing." The corner of Ramón's mouth lifted in a hint of a smirk. "You pulled a few surprise moves on me, too, you know?"

Lori shrugged, acting ambivalent. "Oh, yeah? What's that mean?" she quipped.

"Well, I thought I knew *you,* but I didn't. You never told me about this guy, Devan, or exactly why you two broke up. After getting a restraining order on a crazy former boyfriend, why did you go back for more? A second go-round with a man with mental problems? What were you thinking?"

"I wasn't," Lori admitted, casting her eyes to the floor. In a voice filled with regret, she continued, "I know I should have been upfront with you about Devan, and I admit to a serious lapse in judgment when I agreed to go out with him. However, I was lonely. I was mad at you. And confused."

"Hell, I've been lonely, confused and mad, too, Lori. These past few weeks have been hell."

"They have?"

"Of course. When I came to your birthday party, I planned to beg you to be patient. But then I saw you kissing that guy, and it hurt. It was like a slap in my face, and I didn't feel like getting into it with you, so I left."

Lori slumped down on her spine, toying with her fork. "Kissing Devan to make you jealous was a stupid thing to do. I only did it to make you mad, not run you off. I wanted to give you the impression that I didn't care, when all the time I've really been hurting." A pause passed as Lori looked up at Ramón. "I do care about you...very much. I...I love you, Ramón, and I should have told you long ago, and I should never have started playing games by pulling Devan into our problems."

"Playing games never works," Ramón commented, taking her hand and squeezing her fingers. "I love you, too, Lori, and I'll never let anything happen to you."

Lori could not suppress a grin when she told him, "That was a pretty sneaky move…connecting your cell phone to my outdoor motion sensor without telling me."

"It was. I confess. But it may have saved your life."

Lifting her face to his, she let her gaze linger on Ramón, grateful for the depth of his concern. "Guess I'd better keep you around for 24/7 protection," she joked.

Ramón pressed her palm to his cheek, drew in a long breath and said, "If you'd let me, I'd spend every night sitting in my car outside your house to make sure you're safe."

Lori scooted closer and tilted her forehead against Ramón's. "Don't you think my bed would be a much more comfortable place to sleep?"

With a shift, Ramón guided Lori out of her chair and onto his lap, slipping his arms around her waist. Once she was settled, he cocked his head, as if in question. "Yes, it would, but if you'd like me to stay here with you on a more permanent basis, all you have to do is ask."

"I'm asking," Lori whispered, covering his lips with hers.

Deepening the kiss, Lori arched closer, forcing Ramón to lean back as she plunged her tongue into his mouth to taste every inch of his sweet cavity. While her tongue danced with his, she thrust one hand into the V of his crotch and massaged his unopened package, allowing the friction of her movements to enlarge his member until it fully filled her hand and strained for release.

"Damn, keep that up and you're gonna make me explode all over your kitchen," he groaned against her cheek after breaking off their kiss.

"I'm okay with that," Lori murmured as Ramón reached down and covered her hand with his, adding more pressure to the bulge rising in his pants. When he unbuttoned the waistband of his jeans, slid down the zipper and guided Lori's hand to his firm, throbbing penis, she closed her fingers around his shaft and caressed it with a gentle fist, easing it from its hiding place. Once his manhood was free and standing tall, she made a ring of her thumb and index finger, tightening it around the head of his shaft to tease him with a light steady rub, increasing his arousal as she played her fingers up and down his warm, silky flesh, delighting in the sounds of urgent pleasure coming from Ramón's lips.

"Oh, baby," he murmured. "You don't know what you're doing."

"Oh, yes, I do," she countered with a smile as she moved off his lap and onto her knees to lower her head between his legs. With a few jerks, his jeans came off, along with his briefs, exposing his magnificent tool in all its glory. When Lori tossed his pants across the kitchen, Ramón threw back his head and closed his eyes, giving himself over to Lori's erotic ministrations.

She started with wet kisses across the soft skin of his sack while cradling his testicles in her palm. Using her tongue, she traced lazy half moons atop one, and then the other, applying gentle squeezes with her thumbs as she went. Continuing to make tiny pressure points of sweetness with her lips, Lori inched her way up Ramón's shaft until she reached the head. Using her tongue, she began lapping the tight skin covering the tip, licking his tool as if it were a strawberry lollipop. Her sensuous move made Ramón gasp in delight and press his hands on either side of her face to force her to look up at him. Through smoldering eyes, Lori gazed up at Ramón, her heart full of love for him, her body zinging with desire. She trusted him, believed in their love and knew he was the only man for her. His steadfast devotion, his fierce desire to love and protect her, coupled with their amazing sexual connection, now convinced Lori that they belonged together and were on the path to a new beginning. She'd hidden her true feelings for Ramón for too long, and now she wanted to prove she was fully committed.

Slowly, carefully, she bent lower and drew his erection in between her lips, her mouth wide, her tongue flicking back and forth in a tickling, teasing motion as if he were an ice cream cone about to melt. Wrapping both palms around his base, she pushed him fully into her mouth and sucked him down, moving her head back and forth to feel him swirl around in her mouth, and then quickly let him go.

"Don't stop," Ramón muttered, arching his hips off the chair to present himself more fully to Lori, who chuckled under her breath and resumed her titillating maneuvers. For every light lick of her tongue, she countered with long sucking pulls that brought Ramón to near explosion. She followed shallow taps of

her tongue with intense wet tugs, her lips holding him fast as she explored the ridge around his tip. When she paused long enough to take a breath, Ramón let out a cry of satisfaction that told Lori her exquisite torture was working and her man wanted more.

Closing her mouth around the upper part of his penis, she anchored her hands on Ramón's thighs and settled in, wanting to pleasure him in a way that would take him places he'd never gone before. Drawing hard on his fully erect shaft, she moved her mouth up and down, pumping him as if she were trying to pull a chocolate milkshake through a straw. Stroking downward she sent him deep into her throat. Pulling upward, she dragged him to the point of eruption that she knew he was fighting to control. Curving upward, he arched his back, jammed himself far into her throat, and let out a ragged moan as he sent his sweet love flowing into Lori.

# Chapter 30

Morning came fast. Ramón had no time to linger in bed and extend his sensuous lovemaking with Lori, much as he wanted to. After their erotic tryst in her kitchen yesterday, they'd moved into her bedroom where he'd reciprocated her attention, sexing her to satisfaction as they made up for lost time.

He had reassured her that Xavier's troubles would soon be resolved and that the Mexican authorities, working with Immigration and Customs Enforcement (ICE) were closing in on whoever was helping Lopez smuggle illegal aliens into the States. Very soon, everything would be back to normal and no one would be in danger.

However, Ramón had lost a full day of work yesterday. After making love to Lori, they'd gone to his condo, packed up most of his stuff and moved it into her house. Living with Lori was going to be wonderful and he was excited about this shift in their relationship. At last, she trusted him enough to let her feelings show, and she'd certainly proven the depth of her love for him last night. He wanted to stick around today and help her with the pile of clothing, books and electronic equipment he'd dumped into the corner of her bedroom, but duty called. He had a complicated installation to oversee at a restaurant in Galveston and had to get going before traffic on the Gulf Freeway became a tangled nightmare.

Ramón had showered, dressed and was ready to leave by the time Lori sat up in bed, fully awake. "I'll be on the job all day," he told her, leaning down to give her a peck on the lips. "What's on your agenda?"

"First, I've gotta find space for your things in the spare bedroom closet. Then I'll run by the hardware store and have a key made for you. And then pack. Gotta fill in for Phyllis tomorrow, remember?"

"Right. How long will you be gone this time?"

"Four days."

"Ugh," Ramón groaned, giving her a playful rub on the shoulders. "Just when I move in, you have to leave."

"Give you time to miss me," she joked.

"Thanks, but no thanks," he countered.

"But I will do your laundry, buy groceries and make sure there's food in the house before I leave."

"Gee, you're too good to me," he shot back, stroking her neck with a feathery touch, using the tips of his fingers to titillate her. "First you give me a blow job that blows my mind, and now you're gonna wash my dirty drawers and buy me groceries?"

"Gotta take care of my man," Lori chuckled, tilting back her head to squint up at Ramón through half-closed eyes. "But... this is my move-in special. Don't get too used to it," she added. "After this trip, you're on you own."


By midday, Lori had completed her list of chores. Aware that Brittany had returned home, Lori called her friend and gave her a recap of what had happened while Brittany was in San Francisco.

"Damn. Do you think Devan was going to kill you?" Brittany remarked after hearing about Lori's near attack and Ramón's interception.

"I don't know. Maybe he planned to rape me at knifepoint. Or force me to leave with him. Whatever was on his mind wasn't good. If Ramón hadn't come when he did, I don't know what Devan might have done."

"You're lucky Ramón installed that monitor on his cell phone. He's quite a guy. So, I guess you two are back together?"

"Umm-hmm. We most certainly are," Lori confirmed. "And there've been some changes over here that I think I need to tell you about."

"What's going on?"

"Ramón moved in."

"Really? It's that serious, huh?"

"Well, we're giving it time, but it looks like this might be it for both of us."

"Damn, girl. That's great. I want all the details, but right now I've gotta unpack and make some calls, so why don't we catch up later."

"Will do."

"Okay, but call before six-thirty. Clint's coming over at seven and I don't want to be interrupted, if you know what I mean."

"Sounds like you two are getting pretty tight, too," Lori commented with a laugh.

"It's all good," Brittany replied in a lilting tone. "Tell you more when we talk."

After clicking off, Lori went into her spare bedroom to clean out the closet so Ramón would have some space for his clothes. As she sorted through boxes full of shoes and purses, she smiled. Having Ramón around the house was exactly what she needed to banish that empty feeling that had been plaguing her for weeks. She loved him. He loved her. The future looked brighter than ever.

After organizing the closet, Lori ate a sandwich for lunch at her kitchen counter, and was just about to step into her garage to get another storage box when her cell phone rang. She jumped to get it, hoping Ramón was calling. However, she quickly saw that it was Phyllis.

"Lori! Lori!" Phyllis started right in, sounding very rushed. "Whew! I'm glad I got you."

"Been here all morning. Why? What's up?" Lori asked, surprised by the tension in Phyllis's voice.

"Big change of plans. I have to leave for Seattle today. My sister's had a heart attack!"

"Oh, no. Phyllis, I'm so sorry."

"Can you report to the airport as my emergency replacement today? I'm scheduled to work the midday flight and departure is in ninety minutes."

"Uh, well…" Lori stammered, aware that this was not an unusual request, but one she hadn't been prepared to consider. She'd been looking forward to a quiet evening at home with Ramón as they settled into this new living arrangement, and she'd planned to give him a key. However, she had agreed to help Phyllis out, so stepping in for her a day earlier wasn't too much to ask. Plus, this trip might give Lori a good shot at becoming a crew leader very soon.

"All right. I can do it, Phyllis," Lori replied, her mind spinning ahead to all she had to do. A prepacked flight bag, which she kept ready for times like this, took care of packing. Brittany had a spare key that Ramón could use until Lori returned. As for grocery shopping and doing laundry? Well, Ramón would have to make do on his own.

"Thanks, Lori," Phyllis replied. "Don't bother to call the crew scheduler, I'll arrange it with him. You go get ready."

"I'll be there as soon as I can," Lori replied, disconnecting the call and immediately phoning Brittany to let her know what had come up. "Will you give Ramón your spare key?" she asked. "I've got fifteen minutes to get to the airport. I don't want him to be locked out tonight."

"Sure, no problem," Brittany agreed.

"Great. I'll let him know."

"Have a safe trip," Brittany said.

Lori put on her navy blue and red GAA uniform, tied the standard red and blue striped scarf at her neck, put on her navy low-heeled pumps, and then checked her image in the mirror. Ready to go, she grabbed her flight bag off the shelf in her closet, deciding to phone Ramón from the crew lounge after she'd checked in for her flight assignment.

* * *

Lori entered the parking garage at Bush Intercontinental Airport, parked in her regular spot and popped open the trunk of her car. Rushing around to the back of the vehicle, she bent over, grabbed her bag and slammed the trunk closed. When she turned around, she stopped and screamed. A man was standing there, blocking her path, and he didn't look as if he planned to move.

"Come with me," he ordered, pulling Lori's purse off her shoulder and snatching her flight bag. Taking hold of her arm, he twisted it into her back and forced her toward a black van with heavily tinted windows that was parked right next to her car.

The side door of the van slid open. The man threw her bag inside. Lori struggled to get free, but he gripped her harder and pushed her, headfirst, into the dark vehicle. With her face pressed to the floor, he straddled her, and using a roll of duct tape, quickly bound her hands and feet. When he got off her, Lori flipped over onto her back and used her bound feet to kick out at him.

"Stay down!" he ordered, shoving her back with a slap across her face. Grabbing her by the scarf around her neck, he yanked her face up to his. "Try that again and I'll beat the living crap outta you!" He twisted the scarf until Lori gasped for breath, and then shoved her back down with a grunt.

A bolt of pain ripped through Lori's head when her temple connected with a metal bar in the middle of the floorboard where seats had been removed. She let out the most blood-curdling scream she could manage, praying someone would hear her and realize that she was in trouble.

"You'd better shut up, you stupid bitch!" A woman's harsh voice flew over the front seat and hit Lori like another painful slap.

Astonished, Lori raised her shoulders up off the floor just as the van lurched away with a squeal of tires. Though it was dark in the van, she could see the driver in the rearview mirror, and the sight made her gasp.

*It can't be!* Lori thought, her body going rigid with shock as her eyes connected with those of her coworker, Phyllis Marshall, who was frowning into the mud-streaked windshield, a mean-looking smirk on her lips.

"Phyllis! What are you doing? Why are you here?"

"Just zip your lips and cooperate," Phyllis snapped in a cruel flare that sent shivers of fear through Lori. She had never heard Phyllis, the mild-mannered mother hen, worrywart of the flight crew sound like this. She was the prudent one, the one who rarely left her hotel room during overnights, who never took risks and called Lori naive for daring to step out and experience adventure. How could Phyllis be involved in what was happening to Lori now?

"Who are you, Phyllis? What's happened to you?"

"If you want to see your boyfriend again, you'd better keep quiet and stay down on the floor," was Phyllis's sharp reply.

"My boyfriend?" Lori repeated, incredulous. She groped for answers as the van sped through traffic, her thoughts jarring together as Phyllis took one sharp curve after another at dangerously high speeds. First, Xavier had been threatened in Mexico. Then Ramón was attacked in Houston. And now she was being kidnapped. How did this odd set of circumstances come together? How would it end? With Lori dead or seriously injured?

"What does this have to do with Ramón?" she demanded, not willing to cooperate so easily.

"Didn't I say shut up?" Phyllis screamed, throwing a hard look at the man who was squatting beside Lori. "Do you have her cell phone?"

"Should be right here" was his reply as he rummaged through Lori's purse, pulled out her phone and waved it at Phyllis.

"Good. This better work or Lopez is gonna have both our heads."

"It'll work," the man vowed in a gravely voice. "And when this is over, we'll be rolling in cash."

Phyllis made an unintelligible mutter. "I damn sure hope so, 'cause I ditched my gig at Globus yesterday."

"Ah, well. You've done your part. You earned your share," her cohort said with a sinister sneer that made Lori pull her knees into her stomach and curl into a ball. Lying there, she tried to stop shaking. If she could get control of her nerves, she might be able to think of a way to get out of this jam.

So Phyllis quit GAA? She's working for a man named Lopez? Lori thought, struggling to put the pieces of this scene into place. She recalled what Ramón had told her about the investigation. Lopez must be the ringleader. Could Phyllis be the American connection at the center of the illegal alien-fake birth certificate and official documents scheme? Could she be the informant who told Lopez's men how to get to Ramón?

Lori thought about Ramón's comment on how difficult it was to ever really know a person, and the recollection made her anger flare even more. This was a coworker she had trusted! A woman with whom Lori spent long hours in very close quarters while flying back and forth between two countries. She'd considered Phyllis a friend, maybe not a close one, but close enough to confide in, to have been invited to Lori's birthday party. How could Phyllis have led such a double life without raising suspicion about her involvement in a criminal operation?

"How long have you been doing this?" Lori boldly queried, pushing the limits of Phyllis's threat.

"Long enough to accumulate a nest egg big enough for me to retire yesterday" was her coworker's tart reply.

"So you've been providing information to help illegals get seats on Globus flights so they can enter the States?" Lori ventured, testing her theory out loud.

"How smart of you to figure that out, Lori," Phyllis laughed. "Pretty good for a naive party girl who doesn't care about anything but having a good time."

"That is so untrue. I don't know what you think you're doing, but you'll never get away with this," Lori challenged Phyllis.

"I already have," Phyllis shot back. "Working at Globus allowed me to put together the perfect team to validate passports and create travel documents to make sure the seats Lopez needed were always available. The rest of the team handled the birth certificates, ID cards and social security cards. It was much easier than you'd think."

"What do you plan to do to me?"

"Nothing. You're worthless. It's Ramón Vidal and his brother,

Xavier, who we need, and you, as I think you've guessed by now, are the key. Now, shut up before my friend really has to hurt you."

Silence fell over the van as Lori slumped back and tried to keep still. As they raced through the streets, Lori strained to catch glimpses of street signs and landmarks to get a sense of where they were taking her. Very soon she realized that they were heading south, toward Galveston, where she knew Ramón was working. Deciding her best shot at escape was to act as if she were cooperating, Lori took a deep breath and bit down on her bottom lip, hugging her arms around her sides while trying to stop shaking. They needed *her* to get to Ramón, so they wouldn't harm her too badly, would they? But what did they plan to do to Ramón to make him talk? Lori didn't even want to think about that.

When the van finally rolled to a stop, Lori sat up and peered out the window. Phyllis had parked the vehicle on a wide cement strip that ran along a waterfront pier. Run-down warehouses with gaping holes for windows faced the water. The weatherworn structures resembled tired, ragtag soldiers who had been defeated in battle and were ready for surrender.

Phyllis got out first, followed by her companion, who opened the van door, yanked Lori out and marched her, stumbling, into one of the crumbling buildings.

# Chapter 31

Ramón clicked off his phone, concerned. He'd been trying to get through to Lori all afternoon, with no success. And she hadn't returned any of his messages, either. Her job required her to be accessible by phone for alerts in schedule changes and updated security information, so she rarely turned her cell phone off. What was going on?

*Probably busy trying to get my stuff stowed,* he decided, shrugging off his worries to resume testing the newly installed security cameras he had designed to intercept shoplifters in the Galveston store. However, as he walked from monitor to monitor and adjusted the cameras, he couldn't stop his thoughts from shifting back to Lori. He just hoped she was out buying groceries, planning a great meal that they would enjoy tonight before she departed tomorrow.

When both he and his client were satisfied that the security system was in perfect working order, Ramón left, eager to get home. He got into his truck, but before taking off he tried calling Lori again. No answer. Frustrated, he punched in

Brittany's number, thinking she might know where Lori had been all day.

"Oh, she got called in to work. Emergency duty for Phyllis. Lori asked me to give you my key to her house so you can get in," Brittany informed Ramón.

"When did all this happen? Why didn't she let me know?" Ramón replied, beginning to panic.

"Well, she said Phyllis Marshall called, in a frantic rush, and asked her to work in her place. Some family emergency, I think," Brittany finished.

"But why today?" Ramón threw back, confused. "Lori told me she was going to fill in for Phyllis...but starting tomorrow, not today."

"Umm, I don't know about that," Brittany replied. "Why don't you contact Globus? They'll know which flight she's on. Maybe there was a last-minute change."

"Yeah, but Lori woulda let me know," he murmured, more to himself than to Brittany.

Feeling uneasy about this sudden change of plans, Ramón clicked off and made several calls before he finally got through to Lori's crew scheduler.

"No, Lori wasn't scheduled to fly today," a man with a very high-pitched voice told Ramón, after verifying that Lori had put Ramón Vidal on the list of persons to whom he could release her flight schedule. "And I'm sure she wasn't going to fill in for Phyllis Marshall because Marshall is no longer a Globus-Americas employee."

"What? Are you sure?" Ramón pressed, shocked by this news and wondering why Lori didn't know this.

"Right, but that's all I can tell you," the scheduler said before ending the call.

Ramón sat stunned, fearing the worst. Had Lori been lured out of her house by someone who wanted to hurt her? Not by Devan. He was still in jail. By Lopez's henchmen? They were still out there somewhere. Would they use Lori to make Ramón cooperate with them? If so, she could be in real trouble.

Ramón turned the key in his truck's ignition, accelerated and swung onto the feeder road, heading back toward Houston. What should he do? Go to the airport? To Lori's house to see if she had left him a note? Talk to Phyllis? But he had no idea where Phyllis lived or if she was still in Houston. One way or another, Phyllis Marshall was probably at the center of whatever had happened to Lori.

When Ramón stopped at a red light, he tried to text a message to Xavier but was so worried he kept messing up. The driver behind him leaned on his horn, forcing Ramón to set his cell phone aside and drive on, frustrated as hell. There had to be some connection between what was going on with Lori and the arrest of Lopez, which was set to come off tonight. With some serious investigating and a ton of calls to make, Ramón decided it would be best for him to go to his office, where he would be able to concentrate.

Ramón had just turned onto the street leading to his building when his cell phone rang. He stabbed Talk and listened in shock as a woman told him exactly what he had to do if he ever wanted to see Lori alive again.

"Give up the override codes to access your brother's house and the safe where he's keeping certain documents, and Lori can go free. If not. Well, don't plan on seeing her again."

"I won't agree to anything, *Phyllis*," he shouted, emphasizing her name. When she didn't protest, he knew he'd called it right. "I won't give you a damn thing until you guarantee that Lori is okay," Ramón punched back, letting this crazy woman know he was not about to be intimidated. "For all I know Lori is already seriously hurt...or dead."

"Oh, no. She's right here, looking at me like a frightened little cat," Phyllis assured Ramón.

"I'm coming to see for myself. Where are you?" Ramón demanded.

"Port of Galveston, Pier 6. The old Republic Brewery building."

Ramón snapped off his handheld, gunned his engine and made a fast U-turn to head back toward Galveston. Speeding up the freeway entry ramp, the plan that he and Xavier had devised tumbled around in his head like bits of colored confetti. Would it come off without a hitch?

"It has to," Ramón told himself through tightly clenched teeth, determined to rescue Lori.

The warehouse was dark and filled with trash. It smelled like decayed wood and rusted metal. Using a flashlight that he'd taken from his truck, Ramón swept the area as he crept across the lower floor of the dilapidated structure. The place was eerily quiet. So quiet, he wondered if he had been sent on a wild goose chase—a diversion to buy time. *But why would Lori's captors do that?* he wondered, footsteps echoing through the cavernous building and signaling his arrival to whoever might be lurking in the shadows.

Through the broken windows, Ramón caught glimpses of the dark waters of the Gulf, shimmering gray under the orange glow of an approaching sunset. Only last month, he and Lori had sat on the beach at Acapulco and watched a similarly spectacular sunset slide into the water. At the time, he had drunk in the experience and let it fill him with joy. Now, it sparked nothing but fear and adrenaline. He was not going to let *anything* happen to his woman.

The thump of footsteps overhead jolted Ramón back to the moment. Looking up, he traced a beam of light over the ceiling and then across the room to a spiral staircase, leading to the upper floor. Moving more quickly, he crept up the stairs, entered a narrow corridor and eased down the hallway until he came to a halt near the end. Peering around the corner, Ramón could see directly into a trash-strewn room lit by dim light coming through a dirty window. He saw the same scar-faced man who had attacked him standing beside a woman whose back was to Ramón. It was Phyllis, he knew, recognizing her even from the rear, with her gray-streaked hair and mature, but trim shape. He squinted at the figure, infuriated that Lori's flight crew leader, someone she had trusted, was now holding a gun on the woman he loved.

A shiver of disgust rippled through Ramón, sending a cold wave of anger through him in spite of the heat that blanketed the musty old building. Lori was sitting in a corner, her mouth, hands and feet, wrapped in duct tape, her eyes tensed into slits that were focused on her captors.

"Okay. You wanna talk? Here I am," Ramón boldly announced as he stepped into the room, letting them know that he meant business, would not be intimidated and *was* going to get Lori out alive. He'd caused this, and now he had to fix it.

After rushing into the room, Ramón went straight to Lori, squatted down in front of her and pulled the tape off her mouth.

"Keep her hands tied," Phyllis shouted, glowering at Ramón.

When Lori slumped against him, he held her tight for a quick second and then ignored Phyllis and began to work the bindings off her hands and feet. He could hear her whimpering cries of relief, feel her heart pounding against his shirt and sense the terror that gripped her.

"It's going to be okay," he whispered, stroking her back. "Stay put. Trust me. Trust me, please."

"Get up," the man ordered, forcing Ramón to release Lori when the press of a gun hit the spot between his shoulder blades. "Over there," the scarfaced man demanded, waving his gun toward the far side of the room, where a rickety table and two chairs had been placed beneath the low-hanging rafters of the slanted warehouse roof. A laptop computer and a cell phone lay there, open and ready for use.

Ramón sat down at the table, but shifted around to make sure he could keep an eye on Lori, who remained in the corner. He gave her a quick nod of reassurance to calm her down and let her know that he had control of the situation.

"Watch her," the man yelled at Phyllis before approaching the table to yank out a wooden chair and sit down. He peered with interest at Ramón, as if trying to size him up. "This time, I call the shots," he told Ramón. "You cooperate and this can all be over real fast, you know?" he paused to let his meaning sink in. "It's all up to you, Vidal."

Ramón slowly inclined his head in understanding, cautiously observing the man, whose pitted skin made him look even more menacing than he had when he'd attacked Ramón at his building.

"Start talking," Scarface commanded, suddenly placing his fingers on the keyboard, as if prepared to transmit the information that only Ramón could give him. "And don't give me any fucked-up shit that'll mess this up. I want everything my people in Acapulco need to get past your brother's gates and into the safe, you got me?"

"Yeah," Ramón agreed, sounding very calm. "I'm gonna give you what you need, but first you have to let Lori get up. Let her stand by the door. Once you have what you want, she walks."

The man shrugged, as if he didn't care where Lori went as long as he got what he wanted.

Ramón nodded at Lori, who stood up and went to stand by the open doorway, Phyllis hovering nearby. Next, he leveled a hard stare on the man sitting across from him and said, "The override code to get through the gates is 09568."

Scarface began to type, using his index fingers to tap out the message.

Ramón kept his eyes on Lori while the man typed the code into his computer, not feeling good about the fact that Phyllis was still holding the gun on her. No matter what the man said, Phyllis remained a loose cannon. Who knew what she was capable of doing?

"The house?" the man prompted, waiting.

Ramón's head spun around. "For the house, it's the reverse of those numbers...86590," Ramón divulged.

"Hold on. Not so fast," the man complained, his thick fingers shifting over the keys as he sent the information to whomever was on the other end of the communication.

A brief lull passed while the man waited for a reply and Ramón stared at Lori. Her face was streaked with tears and her eyes were puffy from crying, but she held her chin high, looking defiant and ready to fight. *Good for you, Lori*, Ramón thought. *Don't let these creeps think you've given up because I haven't and I won't. I'm going to get you out of this and it'll all be over real soon.*

"All right. They're inside the house. Now, what about the safe?"

Pulling air though his lips, Ramón took a shudder of a breath and said, "To get into the safe, it's 65294."

"You'd better be telling the truth," the man muttered as he returned to tapping the keyboard, biting his lower lip in concentration.

"I got no reason to lie," Ramón quipped with a roll of his eyes. "But once the safe is open an alarm is gonna sound within ten seconds unless Xavier activates a thumbprint scan." Ramón finished his warning with a smirk on his lips, knowing there was no way for Lopez's men to activate the thumbprint scanner without his help.

"Shit!" Scarface snapped. "A fuckin' thumbprint? What the hell? The judge ain't there!"

Ramón lifted both shoulders, as if to tell him, *I know. And that's your problem, not mine.*

The man lurched across the table and punched Ramón between the eyes, making his nose begin to bleed.

Ramón's right hand shot out. He grabbed the man by his shirtfront and yanked back hard, pulling them nose to nose. "Try that again and I'll kill you."

"Ha!" the man laughed, jerking free. "If any killin' gets done, I'll be doin' it."

Ramón slumped back, wiped the blood from his nose with the back of his hand and clenched his jaw, primed for whatever was coming.

Scarface settled back into his chair, giving his shirt a yank. He raised a brow at Ramón. "You knew crackin' the safe needed a thumbprint and you knew the judge wasn't there."

Ramón nodded, while putting pressure on the bridge of his nose to stop the flow of blood. He wiped his face on the sleeve of his shirt and glared at the man. "Yeah. That's right, Scarface. I knew it. Whatcha gonna do now?" However, what he didn't admit was that the safe could be opened with Ramón's thumbprint, too, if entered along with the numerical code. After meeting with Xavier in Acapulco, the two brothers had decided to set up this extra step, using a biometric security device to authenticate identity based on the physical characteristics of their thumbs. Using the brothers' fingerprints appealed to them as a way to buy time, confuse the thieves and serve as an additional safeguard for Xavier's family. Ramón had installed similar devices many times and knew it would work to slow down access and allow him to implement the rest of his plan. Time was what he and Lori needed most right now.

In a flurry of rage, the man rushed around the table, circled behind Ramón and shoved a gun into the back of Ramón's head. "You better do whatever you gotta do to open that safe, or I pull this goddamn trigger."

Lori started forward, as if to lunge toward Ramón, but only made it a few feet before Phyllis snatched her back and shoved her down onto her knees. "You'd better *not* interfere," Phyllis warned Lori, jamming her foot into Lori's back and holding her down on the splintery wooden floor.

"All right, all right," Ramón conceded, alarmed by the grunts of pain coming from Lori's lips. "It's set to take my left thumbprint, too."

"So? What do I gotta do?" the man snapped.

"Scan my thumbprint into your computer and send it to your boys in Acapulco. If they're smart, they'll open the image on a cell phone, place it over the scanner on the safe and it'll work."

"It better," Lopez shot back, grabbing Ramón's left hand and jamming it onto his computer screen. He pressed Scan, sent the image through and then typed in the override code again.

For the next five minutes, no one spoke. Ramón cautiously watched Lori and Phyllis, while Scarface returned to jam his gun against the back of Ramón's head. When the abductor's cell phone beeped, he grabbed his handheld and scowled at the screen. "It went through," he told Phyllis. "They got in the safe and have the documents." He jerked his head toward the door. "Get her outta here, while I take care of this one."

Phyllis snatched Lori by the arm, yanked her to her feet, and shoved her out the door, leaving Ramón alone with Phyllis's accomplice.

Lori walked haltingly, her knees nearly buckling as she held onto the rickety railing for support and descended the rusty steps.

As hard as it was to keep up her courage, she knew she could not falter. Ramón had come through for her. He'd managed to get her out alive, but what about him? Somehow, Lori had to distract Phyllis, and go back to help Ramón.

Stumbling out of the warehouse, Lori resisted Phyllis's insistent prodding as the two women walked toward the van. However, as soon as Phyllis pulled back the sliding door and turned around to push Lori inside, she knew what to do. Drawing on the survival training she had taken during flight attendant school, she whipped around and lodged a gut-wrenching kick to Phyllis's stomach, landing a hard punch that sent the woman to her knees and the handgun flying across the cement. After another hard kick to Phyllis's side, Lori bent down and twisted Phyllis's right arm behind her back, causing the woman so much pain she collapsed in tears and screamed for Lori to let her go.

With Phyllis down, Lori tied her up with some of her leftover duct tape, grabbed the gun and sprinted back toward the warehouse, desperate to help Ramón.

Ramón slid both hands under the table, but kept his eyes locked on Scarface. After flattening his palms on the underside of the table, he silently counted to five and then upended it with a firm push, crashing it against his captor's head.

"What the fuck?" Scarface shouted, flailing his arms as he heaved the splintered furniture aside. Furious, he stalked toward Ramón, who in the confusion of the moment managed to race across the room and come up behind Scarface to wrap one arm around the man's neck.

Scarface struggled to get free, but Ramón held on fast. Using all the strength he could muster, Ramón squeezed his assailant's neck with one arm while trying to dislodge the weapon that the thug still held in his right hand. Scarface jerked back. Ramón increased the pressure until he heard the gun clatter to the floor. Not wasting a second, Ramón quickly bent down to grab it, letting go of Scarface, who fled toward the stairs.

With the weapon cupped in his palm, Ramón raised the gun, narrowed his eyes at the fleeing man and fired.

Just as Lori was about to reenter the warehouse, two sounds stopped her in her tracks. She tensed, terrified by the crack of a gunshot, yet relieved to hear the shrill of a police car siren in the distance.

# *Chapter 32*

Lori raced up the stairs toward Ramón, and screamed as soon as she reached the top step, which was blocked by the body of the scar-faced man. He was lying on the floor, blood streaming from his stomach, while Ramón stood over him holding his wrist with blood seeping between his fingers.

"Oh, no!" Lori cried out, shocked by the bloody scene.

"Looks worse than it is," Ramón reassured her, linking his good arm through hers to pull her close. "Yeah, I shot the guy. He's dead. But my bullet ricocheted off a metal pipe and struck *me* in the hand."

Lori examined Ramón's wound. "This looks bad."

"Could be worse. At least this is all over," Ramón told Lori as they exited the building and approached a paramedic who immediately began tending to Ramón's wounded hand.

Lori checked the area and spotted Phyllis sitting in the back of a patrol car, her head lowered so that Lori couldn't see her coworker's face. *How sad*, Lori thought. She had really liked Phyllis. *You never really know people*, Ramón had told her. *Boy, was he right.*

"Hey, Ramón. It worked out just like we planned," a police officer remarked as he approached. "Lopez and four of his men, all part of his ring, are on their way to jail in Acapulco."

Lori jerked around and glared at Ramón, clearly confused. "What's that mean? My kidnapping was staged?" She could feel her anger rising, her disappointment in Ramón gathering steam. "Ramón, don't you dare tell me that…"

"Shh," Ramón hissed, shaking his head. "No. None of what happened tonight was actually planned. However, Xavier and I did work out a way to make sure the thugs in Acapulco would be arrested as soon as they tried to get into his safe."

"How?" Lori probed, still not certain she could believe what he told her.

"Well, it's like this," Ramón started, going on to tell Lori what he and Xavier had done. "We set up the thumbprint code to serve as a signal to the authorities. I designed the alarm to simultaneously alert the police in Houston and in Acapulco if either Xavier or I tried to access the safe using the biometric device. So, once my thumbprint scan went through and was used to open the safe, that notified the authorities in both countries that it was time to move in."

"But how did the police find us tonight?" Lori asked, still reeling from all the information Ramón was throwing at her.

"They found us through the GPS in my cell phone, which was connected to the silent alarm."

"And where is Xavier? Carmen and Linda?" Lori wanted to know.

"They're safe in my condo in Houston, waiting for my all-clear call."

"So, that's why you wanted to move in with me? To make room for Xavier and his family to move into your place?"

Ramón looked down at Lori, kissed her on the nose and chuckled. "Not at all, though it did work out real well. I moved in with you because I love you, want to protect you and adore the way we make love."

Lori slapped playfully at Ramón, both thankful and frustrated by the outcome of the most dangerous incident she had ever been involved in. Even her run-in with Devan hadn't been this serious. "Why didn't you clue me in on what you were up to?" she demanded, sounding rather cross.

"Because I promised not to drag you further into mine and Xavier's troubles, didn't I?"

With a sigh, Lori inclined her head in agreement. How could she fault Ramón for taking such risks to protect his brother's family, and her as well? When he took her in his arms, she went limp in relief. She was proud of him. In love with him. And convinced that he would never crowd her or try to clip her wings. He was a first-class guy, the man she wanted to love forever.

# *Epilogue*

One week after the incident, Lori snuggled down into her seat beside Ramón in the first-class cabin aboard Globus-Americas Airlines flight 677, bound for Rio de Janeiro. Ramón braced his arm, which was still in a sling, against the cabin window, while Lori rested her head on his shoulder.

"We're about to take off. Anything else I can do for you?" asked the attractive flight attendant who had been helping them get settled. When she leaned low over their seats, Lori glanced up at the woman, who was looking straight past Lori and into Ramón's eyes, as if he were sitting there all alone. Lori huffed her irritation, but smiled at the attendant who'd been doting on Ramón ever since they boarded.

"Thanks, but he's fine," she answered for Ramón, using as cordial a tone as she could manage.

"Well, don't hesitate to call me if you need *anything,*" the attendant remarked, eyes riveted on Ramón.

"I appreciate your offer, but *I* can handle things from here," Lori replied, leaning into the attendant's line of vision to make her point.

Ramón shook his head and grinned at Lori after the woman turned and walked away. "That wasn't very nice."

"What? It's true. I'm perfectly capable of taking care of my man without help from her."

"You've got that right," Ramón repeated, giving Lori a kiss that intensified as the plane ascended into the clouds.

As soon as the plane leveled off, Ramón leaned back and closed his eyes while Lori reviewed the brochure that detailed the amenities of their hotel in Rio.

"Guess what?" she began, giving Ramón a gentle nudge.

"What?" he murmured, not opening his eyes.

"The club at our hotel has a great dance floor. Looks out over the ocean. A lot like Club Azule."

Ramón looked over at Lori, raised an eyebrow and then lifted his injured arm.

"That's nice, but I doubt we'll be doing much dancing for a while."

Lori gave him a slow seductive grin and snuggled closer. "That's okay. For once, I'm actually looking forward to sticking around the hotel room."

"Really?"

"Yeah. And I plan to show you some moves that I definitely couldn't throw down on a dance floor."

"I can hardly wait," Ramón replied, easing his lips over hers.

\* \* \* \* \*